ROBLOX

EGMONT
We bring stories to life

First published in Great Britain 2018, by Egmont UK Limited
The Yellow Building, 1 Nicholas Road
London W11 4AN

Written by Alexander Cox
Edited by Craig Jelley and Jacqui Butler
Designed by John Stuckey and Andrea Philpots
Illustrations by Ryan Marsh, John Stuckey and Joe Bolder
Special thanks to the entire Roblox team

ISBN 978 1 4052 9161 3

68557/001
Printed in China

Spending time online is great fun! Here are a few simple rules to help younger fans stay safe
and keep the internet a great place to spend time. For more advice and guidance, please see
page 144 of this book, or go to www.connectsafely.org/Roblox.

- Never give out your real name – don't use it as your username.
- Never give out any of your personal details.
- Never tell anybody which school you go to or how old you are.
- Never tell anybody your password except a parent or guardian.
- Be aware that you must be 13 or over to create an account on many sites. Always check
the site policy and ask a parent or guardian for permission before registering.
- Always tell a parent or guardian if something is worrying you.

ROBLOX

CHARACTER ENCYCLOPEDIA

INTRODUCTION

Welcome to the Roblox Character Encyclopedia – a jam-packed collection of the most awesome, most legendary and most popular characters that make up the community.

You can learn all about the creators behind smash-hit games like Jailbreak, Apocalypse Rising and MeepCity, or meet the weird and wacky cast that makes up the Roblox Family. You can even discover famous social media stars that live, breathe and make videos on Roblox, who you can follow for more bloxy adventures.

The characters are arranged in alphabetical order, so you can easily find your favourite Robloxian, but if you're interested in a particular type of character, use the contents below.

❘ CONTENTS

INFLUENCERS

ROBLOX CLASSIC

CREATORS

1X1X1X1

SCOURGE OF THE FOURTH DIMENSION, WORSE THAN URBAN LEGENDS TELL

An ancient, extra-dimensional malevolence of truly unspeakable power, 1x1x1x1 despises all things three-dimensional and will stop at nothing to bring about their destruction. Often imitated, but never equalled by those who seek to create chaos, there are many who believe 1x1x1x1 is simply an urban legend or myth.

ROBLOX FAMILY CHARACTER

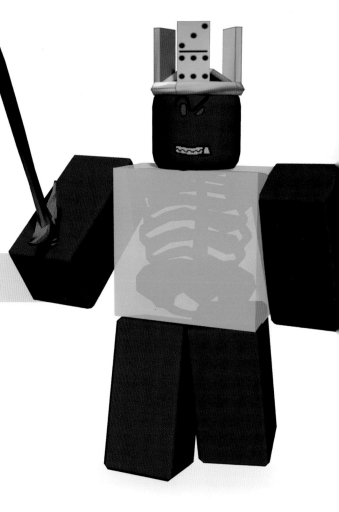

DARKHEART

SKELETON TORSO

PLANNING TO DESTROY THE WORLD IN ... MONSTER ISLANDS

The enigmatic 1x1x1x1 likes to spend his downtime embroiled in a little bit of troublesome game-playing. His favourite is TheSteelEagle's Monster Islands, where he teams up with lesser beings to take on hordes of indescribable horrors across numerous islands. Not even the super-powerful bosses can match 1x1x1x1's evil.

GAME STATS

DEVELOPER
TheSteelEagle

Monster Islands is the first big game from TheSteelEagle and it was initially released back in 2009. Over 7 million fans have joined forces to battle against the invading Monster Forces since its inception.

VISITED

FAVOURITED

AESTHETICAL

MULTI AWARD-WINNING DEV, WHO'S THE EPITOME OF A SNAPPY DRESSER

Aesthetical is the grand-warden of Robloxian social play. This tank-top-wearing developer is known for his break-out game Prison Life, which has been played over 700 million times! Aesthetical stole the show at the 4th Annual Bloxy Awards in 2017, escaping the ceremony with three awards for most mobile visitors, most mobile concurrents and most visitors overall.

CREATOR

HMMM FACE

MUSICA FRIGIDUS DOMINATOR

DEVELOPER TIMELINE

JANUARY 2014
Aesthetical made a New Year's resolution to play and create awesome games and set about following through on his promise by joining Roblox on New Year's Day.

ROBLOX

JAN 2014

SEPTEMBER 2016
Version 2.0 of Prison Life was released, adding a motley collection of new features, a fully redesigned prison and polishing the graphics to an exceptional standard.

PRISON LIFE
GUARDS   PRISONERS

Join guards   Join Prisoners

MAY 2014
Mere months after he signed up, Aesthetical was ready to launch the legendary escape game, Prison Life – which is still one of the most played games on Roblox.

FEBRUARY 2017
Prison Life was awarded a triad of titles at the 4th annual Bloxy Awards. Aesthetical's avatar now proudly carries around one of the glittering trophies.

ALAR KNIGHT OF THE SPLINTERED SKIES

PARAGON OF THE SKY, PROTECTOR OF THE GREAT REALM BELOW

Many centuries ago, the Knights of the Splintered Skies discovered the power of flight and founded a great kingdom in the sky. Sworn to defend the peace and honour of Robloxia, Alar Knight of the Splintered Skies now watches from his sky-high battlements, ready to descend and fight any evil horde that dares to threaten the great realm below.

ROBLOX FAMILY CHARACTER

ALAR KNIGHT OF THE SPLINTERED SKIES HELMET

SWORD OF THE EPIC BLUENESS

BATTLING FOR GLORY IN ... IMPERIUM

Alar Knight of the Splintered Skies has taken the knight's oath of honour and is neither able nor willing to break the code of chivalry, so even when he's off duty, he's still on-code playing the medieval RPG classic Imperium. After a busy day on the battlements, he enjoys nothing better than a bit of wood chopping, warmongering and good old-fashioned feudalism.

GAME STATS

DEVELOPER
Imperator

Imperium was created by Roytt, a developer known for showcases such as Shiver and Wheaten Valley. His games are released through the Imperator group, including his most recent effort, Beyond The Stars.

VISITED

FAVOURITED

ALEXNEWTRON

MULTI-TALENTED CREATOR WITH A PENCHANT FOR SPORTS AND CITY SIMS

The true Roblox Dodgeball champion of champions, Alexnewtron has become a technical master of the sporting challenge! When he's not sending players to Ouchtown with his dodgeball skills, he's hard at work developing other awesome Roblox experiences, most notably his social hangout masterpiece MeepCity, which is one of the most played games on Roblox.

BUBBLE FACE

WHITE BANDED RED TOP HAT

CREATOR

DEVELOPER TIMELINE

DECEMBER 2007
As the year came to a close, Alexnewtron discovered the wonderful world of Roblox and joined its ever increasing community of gamers and creators.

MARCH 2015
He first released his energetic hit-and-dodge classic DODGEBALL! and has accumulated over 43 million visits from world-class dodgers since.

AUGUST 2011
He won the Builder of the Year award at the first ever Roblox Rally, where gamers, staff and developers gathered to discuss all things Roblox.

FEBRUARY 2016
He released his most successful game to date, MeepCity, which has had over 1 billion visits. It's full of dozens of amazing minigames.

APOCALYPSE RISING: SURVIVOR

BORN INTO THE HUSK OF A WORLD, HE KNOWS HOW TO DO ONE THING ...

Few things are more annoying than an end-of-the-world abloxalypse, and even fewer people are equipped to survive it! Apocalypse Rising: Survivor is one of those people. Born into a world that demands endurance, he knows where to find food and water, what places work as super-secure bases and, most importantly, he knows how to kick butt when bandits come knocking!

FRENCH BRIMMED CAP

DARING BEARD

EATING A CAN OF BEANS IN ... APOCALYPSE RISING

GAME INFORMATION

Survivor hails from the massively popular Apocalypse Rising from Gusmanak and ZolarKeth. This open-world survival game pits players against undead droves and rival crews to hunt for the basic life necessities – food, water – and survive! With several huge maps, a wealth of weapons and an awesome atmospheric soundtrack, this tense and addictive survival game has attracted over 175 million visits to date.

DEVELOPER
Gusmanak (p. 51)

VISITED

FAVOURITED

ASIMO3089

ACCLAIMED DEVELOPER WHO PUTS THE 'IMO' IN BADIMO

A debonair developer who possesses as much substance as style, asimo3089 knows how to look good and create intricate Roblox experiences. Over his nine-year career on Roblox he has crafted a canon of much-loved games and showcases, such as The Wind and Roadrunner Canyon, which have earned him several awards including the much-coveted Builder of the Year.

TIMELESS TOP HAT

WANWOOD SWORD CANE

CREATOR

DEVELOPER TIMELINE

DECEMBER 2009

He began work on his first Roblox creation, Scattered, which was originally created during a 4-hour game-jam challenge! That's a lot of game in such a little time.

JANUARY 2017

He started work on the bars, bricks and mortar of Badimo's break-out hit, Jailbreak, which became the first Roblox game ever to hit 3 million favourites.

JUNE 2014

asimo3089 won the much-coveted Builder of the Year at BLOXcon 2014, which saw over 125,000 Robloxians tune in to watch the six-hour-long stream.

QUICK FACT

asimo3089 joined forces with programmer badcc to create the super development group Badimo.

AZUREWRATH, LORD OF THE VOID

NEFARIOUS MENACE FROM THE DARKEST OF DIMENSIONS

Bow down and worship his magnificence or forever be imprisoned in his eternal void of darkness! As evil as his heart is black, Azurewrath, Lord of the Void, uses his vile powers and magical dagger to destroy anyone who dares try to tame his wrath or hinder his malevolent master plans. He is unmatched by the ordinary Robloxian.

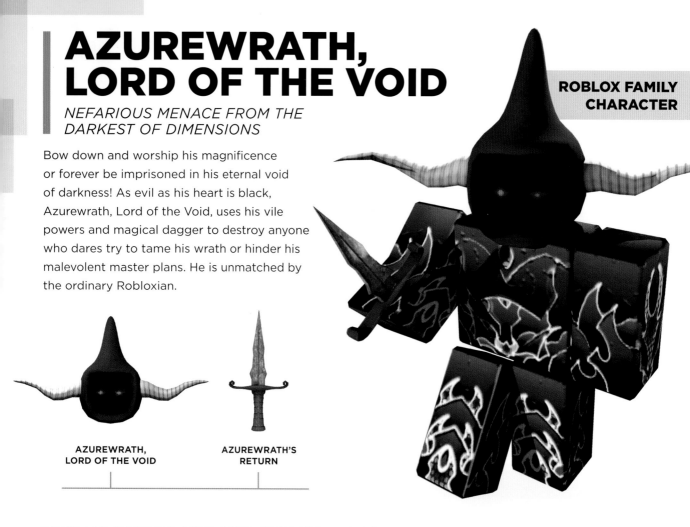

AZUREWRATH, LORD OF THE VOID

AZUREWRATH'S RETURN

UNLEASHING HIS WRATH IN ... MOUNT OF THE GODS

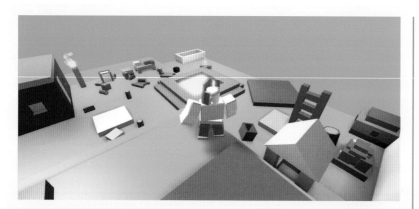

When Azurewrath, Lord of the Void, is in need of a little downtime from lording it over his abyss of darkness, he pays a visit to the mythical masterpiece Mount of the Gods. He hangs up his own god complex at the door, puts on his comfiest apparel and settles into his favourite chair to embark on an afternoon of servitude, lava pits, ritual sacrifice ... and a spot of gardening.

GAME STATS

DEVELOPER

Wheatlies

Mount of the Gods is a co-op survival game created by Wheatlies and DoogleFox. They released the god sim in 2016 and over 13 million visitors have dropped by to appease their respective deities.

VISITED

FAVOURITED

BEEISM

MASTER BUILDER, COLLABORATOR AND DEVELOPER IN HER OWN RIGHT

Buzzing builder Beeism's mantra is reflected in her graceful creations that have a sting in the tail! When she's not a hive of activity working on her Roblox experience From the Deep, she commands a vast, unstoppable army of adorably fussy honeybees, who will stop at nothing to appease their magnificent queen.

CREATOR

PRANKSTER

EARL OF THE FEDERATION

DEVELOPER TIMELINE

JUNE 2015
Beeism began her career by contributing to taymaster's survival fighting game, Twisted Murderer, by building an awesome map set in a bowling alley.

DECEMBER 2017
She contributed a number of builds to the deep-sea action game, From the Deep, which will be released by the developers of the From The Deep group.

FEBRUARY 2016
Beeism released the frantic brawler, Demented Defense, as part of the development group Team Demented. It's since gained well over 900,000 visits.

QUICK FACT
As well as being a top dev, Beeism also helps to test games, like Heroes of Robloxia by MasterOfTheElements.

BEREZAA

MASTER OF THE TYCOON GENRE, WITH PLENTY OF GAMES UNDER HIS BELT

Renowned for his tycoon games, berezaa has built himself a stellar career as an all-star developer. Since joining Roblox in 2009, he has created a collection of popular sim games that include Azure Mines, Miner's Haven and 2 Player Gun Factory Tycoon, all of which have accumulated more than 100 million visits!

CREATOR

BEAUTIFUL HAIR FOR BEAUTIFUL PEOPLE

ARCTIC COMMANDO

DEVELOPER TIMELINE

JUNE 2014
berezaa started work on his first simulation game on the Roblox platform, 2 Player Gun Factory Tycoon, which has attracted over 48 million visits to date.

JUNE 2016
Seemingly mine-crazy, berezaa created the addictive mine-and-build game Azure Mines, which contains a massive randomly generated cave system.

JUNE 2015
He released the beta version of his classic sim Miner's Haven, which would later become Miner's Haven Resurrected, an updated version released in 2017.

FEBRUARY 2017
He left the 4th Annual Bloxys with two awards, including one for Community Excellence for his game Miner's Haven, almost two years after release.

BLOGGIN ALL CATS

FRIENDLY TO ALL LUCKY ENOUGH TO ENCOUNTER HER, BUT ESPECIALLY TO FELINES

Bloggin All Cats is smitten with just about any kitten that shows up on her Robloxian doorstep. One of her main hobbies, aside from taking hundreds of feline photos for her blog, is to kit-knit cute little sweaters for her furry friends. Bloggin All Cats is the ultimate cat woman ... she didn't choose the cat life, the cat life chose her.

ROBLOX FAMILY CHARACTER

FROM THE VAULT:
KAWAII CAT

KITTY EARS

TAKING SELFIES WITH KITTENS IN ... ROBLOXIA ZOO

When this cat-lover is without her furry four-legged friends – and that is a very rare occasion indeed – she still finds a way to play with her animal pals by logging on to Robloxia Zoo. She can peruse the exhibits at her leisure, or fulfil her lifelong dream to actually become an animal! She can choose between lizards, horses, monkeys and more, but she will always opt for the biggest cat of them all – the fearsome lion.

GAME STATS

DEVELOPER
Mimi_Dev

This Bloxy Award-winning dev opened the doors to her zoo sim in 2012. She's also known for her dancing game, Dance Your Blox Off, which she co-created with dev partner DarthChadius.

VISITED

FAVOURITED

BLUE LAZER PARKOUR RUNNER

*ARMED TO THE TEETH AND ABLE TO
HOLD HER OWN AGAINST THE BEST*

They said never bring a sword to a gun fight. So instead,
she brought both. Blue LAZER Parkour Runner is never
one to follow the rules, and she breaks them with grace
and style in the awesome fighting game LAZER. Don't
underestimate this free-running fighter – the fiery blue
flames on her outfit indicate she can be too hot to handle!

**GAME
CHARACTER**

ANIMAZING HAIR

**PURPLE SUPER
HAPPY JOY**

WALL-JUMPING IN ... LAZER

GAME INFORMATION

This free-running fighter is inspired by the
action-packed LAZER, created by lead developer
MasterOfTheElements. In LAZER, players
compete in an arena where they can show
off their parkour skills, as well as their deadly
marksmanship. With different modes, including
Last Man Standing and Capture the Flag, plus
a range of maps and an armoury of weapons,
LAZER is a true challenge for any combat gamer.

DEVELOPER
MasterOfTheElements

VISITED

FAVOURITED

BLUESTEEL WARRIOR

THE LAST IN A LONG LINE OF WARRIORS TO ASSUME A LEGENDARY MANTLE

Many eons ago, the acclaimed title of Bluesteel Warrior was only bestowed upon those who had proved themselves to be the worthiest of all noob-slayers. Now in Robloxia, a new combatant has emerged from the fighting ranks of old and been crowned the Bluesteel Warrior, ready to battle any foe – noob or veteran – that stands in his way.

ROBLOX FAMILY CHARACTER

THE BLUESTEEL BATHELM

IMMORTAL SWORD: THE PIECE MAKER

HUNTING DOWN UNSUSPECTING TARGETS IN ... ASSASSIN!

Bluesteel Warrior can't get enough of living life on the cutting edge, so he leads a double life – noob-slayer by day, seasoned hitman by night, playing the ultimate fighting game, Assassin!. It's the perfect environment to road-test his inordinate warrior stealth and precise close-combat techniques, with an arsenal of cool customised knives to earn, use and treasure.

GAME STATS

DEVELOPER
prisman

Released in 2016, Assassin! has already gained more than a million favourites and over 330 million visits, making the sneaky brawler the jewel in purple-clad programmer prisman's game development crown.

VISITED

FAVOURITED

BOY GUEST

EXPLORING AN EXCITING NEW WORLD FOR THE FIRST TIME

ROBLOX FAMILY CHARACTER

It may be his first outing on Roblox, but fear not, he's a really quick learner and eager to impress! The perfect guest for any Robloxian host to take under their wing, Boy Guest is keen to make new friends and loves playing new games or meeting new Robloxians who are willing to guide him through his Roblox adventures!

BOY GUEST FACE

RED ROBLOX CAP

VISITING HIS FAVOURITE LANDMARKS IN ... WORLD EXPEDITION

He's new in town, and Boy Guest can't wait to see the wonderful world of Roblox, so the logical first stop on his epic gaming trek is the globetrotting showcase World Expedition. With a ticket to fly and a snazzy purple suitcase in tow, he can breeze through security with ease, choose a destination and explore the world without ever leaving his home ... if he can make his flight in time!

GAME STATS

DEVELOPER
legoseed

Over 12 million Robloxians have packed their bags and boarded flights at Roblox International Airport in World Expedition, which is developer legoseed's first release on Roblox.

VISITED

FAVOURITED

BRIDE

*SHE SAID YES TO THE DRESS,
THE TIARA AND THE FLOWERS ...*

She's going to the chapel and she's going to get married! The angelic Bride is a sight to behold, adorned with an opulent crown and clothed in a beautiful dress made from the finest Robloxian fabrics. She looks beautiful dressed as a bride, but you won't always find her in white ...

**BEAUTIFUL BLOND HAIR
FOR BEAUTIFUL PEOPLE**

BRIDE TIARA

CRUSHING THE COMPETITION IN ... DESIGN IT!

GAME INFORMATION

... other times she's setting trends with awesome new looks in Design It!. From the mind of developer tktech, this game has been visited over 140 million times since 2016. Players are given a theme, a budget and five minutes to rummage through the wardrobes to come up with an eye-catching look. When the last tick has tocked, it's time to walk the walk on the Design It! stage, where competitors vote for the best outfit!

DEVELOPER
tktech

VISITED

FAVOURITED

BRIGHTEYES

GUARDIAN OF THE CATALOG AND EMPRESS OF ALL ACCESSORIES

BrightEyes is full of bright ideas and her brightest by far is the Roblox Catalog! This bloxy entrepreneur has set her sights on building the ultimate virtual goods empire, filled with a limitless supply of sensational shirts and hats, and aisles of awesome accessories. She's the complete fashionista and doesn't just stock the best threads, she wears them too!

ROBLOX CLASSIC

BRIGHTEYES FABULOUS HAIR

80S CHECKERBOARD SHUTTER SHADES

ONE OF HER FAVOURITE GAMES IS ... CATALOG HEAVEN

BrightEyes likes to see things dazzle and shine ... which is exactly what she does in Sky Studios' Catalog Heaven. BrightEyes gets to delve deep into her virtual-goods empire and outfit herself in the latest threads, gear and weapons so she can go forth and battle! Being the empress of accessories, she also has super-special VIP status and the ultimate gamepass so she can access the most powerful items!

GAME STATS

DEVELOPER

Sky Studios

Catalog Heaven has netted the super-dev team Sky Studios more than 160 million visits since it was first released in 2010, making it one of the most visited places in all Robloxia!

VISITED

FAVOURITED

BUCK-EYE THE PIRATE

BRAZEN BUCCANEER WITH AS MANY SECRETS AS TREASURE CHESTS

A-harrr! Watch out or he'll keelhaul you all! A swashbuckling scallywag with a fondness for all things piratey, Buck-Eye the Pirate is the mischievous scourge of the Neverland Lagoon. In the open-world adventures of the classic Roblox role-play game, Buck-Eye the Pirate will stop at nothing to protect his ultimate pirate booty ... The Lost Treasure of the Mermaids!

GAME CHARACTER

RUBYHORDE THE RAPACIOUS'S TREASURE

PIRATE ZOMBIE

HANGING WITH HIS MATEYS IN ... NEVERLAND LAGOON

GAME INFORMATION

Buck-Eye the Pirate can be found hanging around open-world fantasy Neverland Lagoon. You better polish up on your pirate-talk because this swashbuckler isn't easily fooled. He has found a huge haul of treasure, and he's not going to tell any old seadog where to find it. Neverland Lagoon is a massively popular Roblox role-play game and has attracted more than 24 million visits to its fantastical world.

DEVELOPER

SelDraken (p. 113) and Teiyia (p. 127)

VISITED

FAVOURITED

BUILDERMAN

THE ROBLOX PIONEER WHO INSPIRED MILLIONS TO IMAGINE AND CREATE

As the original avatar used by Roblox CEO, David Baszucki, Builderman serves as an icon for the tremendous possibilities on Roblox and continues to spark the imagination of all aspiring creators. As a chief founding member of Roblox, he is on a journey to create the ultimate Imagination Platform. So far, over 500 million people have signed up on Roblox and have followed in Builderman's footsteps, both as players and as creators.

MR. CHUCKLES

HARD HAT

ROBLOX FAMILY CHARACTER

David has been at the helm of Roblox since 2004, when the beta was launched in collaboration with co-founder Erik Cassel. The platform was originally called Dynablocks, but was rebranded a year later to the Roblox we know and love. When it originally launched, there were only three games available and limited customisation, but it soon began to grow exponentially.

From playing with construction toys to building physics engines and new tools for game creation, David has always aspired to power the imaginations of kids across the world. With the support of his team and millions of Robloxians, his Imagination Platform has helped usher in the next generation of entertainment spanning across PCs, mobile devices, consoles and VR.

As Builderman, David had a hand in creating lots of Roblox's earliest games, along with fellow Robloxians Erik Cassel, John Shedletsky and Matt Dusek. These games have been visited thousands of times. Although they're no longer accessible, they're still visible on Builderman's profile if you need some inspiration from one of the original Robloxians.

BUSINESS CAT

FURRY ENTREPRENEUR WITH GREEDY PAWS IN MANY PIES

Business Cat isn't kitten around! When he says those TPS reports are urgent, you had better jump on it because he wants them on his desk right meow! This Business Cat is leader of the pride and likes everything to be purrfect, otherwise the claws come out and the whole office will be back, working hard on a Cat-urday!

PARTY EXECUTIVE BRIEFCASE

BUSINESS CAT

LOVES MAKING MONEY IN ... THEME PARK TYCOON 2

Every day is a work day for this corporate cat, and every play can be turned into a money-making opportunity, so it is no surprise that Business Cat likes to mix business with pleasure in Theme Park Tycoon 2. He gets to build his own theme park full of money-spinning burger joints, pizza places and soda stands, plus a few rides, of course. Customer satisfaction comes second to the dollar bills, though.

GAME STATS

DEVELOPER
Den_S

Theme Park Tycoon 2 is packed full of customisable building fun. It has even earned its creative developer Den_S several Bloxy Awards, including the much-coveted Builderman Award of Excellence.

VISITED

FAVOURITED

CAPTAIN RAMPAGE

RAMPAGE IS HIS NAME, PLUNDERING IS HIS GAME

Tales tell of the thousand battles Captain Rampage fought and survived across land and sea. The fearless Captain is renowned for keeping his mateys close, but his treasure even closer. Plunderers and marauders should be very careful – if a foe should be so foolish as to cross him, he'll gladly offer them a long walk off a short plank, on a one-way trip to Davy Jones' locker!

ROBLOX FAMILY CHARACTER

CAPTAIN RAMPAGE SWORD

CAPTAIN RAMPAGE'S PIRATE HAT

PLUNDERING AND PILLAGING IN ... TRADELANDS

Being a fearsome pirate, the Captain loves games that send him on new high-seas adventures without the need to leave his booty unattended and open for looting. Tradelands offers a glut of galleons in which to set sail, and plenty of treasure to collect and trade with other ocean-faring pirates. And if the wind blows the right way, the Captain could find himself in a good old-fashioned cannon fight!

GAME STATS

DEVELOPER
Nahr_Nahrstein

Over 19 million players have adopted the pirate lifestyle in Tradelands, a swashbuckling adventure game from the imagination of moustachioed developer Nahr_Nahrstein.

VISITED

FAVOURITED

CHEF

MEET THE MAN WHO'S BEEN SERVING UP SUPER SLICES SINCE 2008

Olive oil courses through his veins, his muscles are made of pure mozzarella and his culinary skills are the 'sauce' of many legends. He is the man, the myth ... the Pizza Chef! He can normally be found in the hectic kitchen of Builder Brothers Pizza, pounding dough, ladling on lashings of sauce and dishing out generous helpings of the tastiest toppings.

GAME CHARACTER

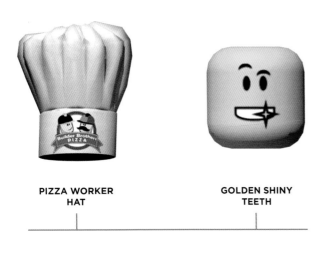

PIZZA WORKER HAT

GOLDEN SHINY TEETH

BRINGING THE HEAT IN ... SNIPER CITY

GAME INFORMATION

This legendary foodie hails from Dued1's Work at a Pizza Place. When he's not tossing around dough, he enjoys chilling at his place and playing his second-favourite Dued1 game, Sniper City. He loves challenging other pizza lovers to a game of stealth and long-range marksmanship. Players are dropped into a high-rise sniper battle, where they must keep one eye on their targets and the other on their health!

DEVELOPER
Dued1 (p. 38)

VISITED

FAVOURITED

CHICKEN MAN

CRISPY, DELICIOUS AND ABSOLUTELY CUCKOO ABOUT CHICKEN

Infused with the power of poultry, this clucky Robloxian is on an epic quest to find the greatest treasure known to chickenkind. On his journey, Chicken Man must overcome fowl-play, cross roads and decipher the secret recipe in his search for the perfectly crisp and exquisitely moist elixir of ultimate power ... the fabled Golden Chicken Leg!

ROBLOX FAMILY CHARACTER

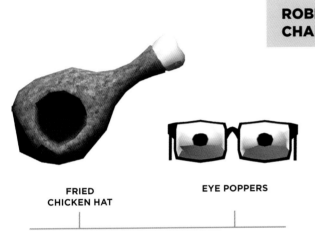

FRIED CHICKEN HAT

EYE POPPERS

GOING CUCKOO FOR POULTRY IN ... SKYBLOCK 2

Chicken Man is brimming with clucky creativity, so it's no surprise his go-to game is the island-building sim Skyblock 2, where he can fly up to the clouds – a skill that only he possesses among chickenkind – and create an idyllic floating paradise. He can't get enough of chopping trees and harvesting; he loves his little farm, complete with – you guessed it – plenty of chickens!

GAME STATS

DEVELOPER

Ultraw

Skyblock 2 is one of developer Ultraw's many popular building sims. Ultraw is also the main scripter for the game-creation group UltraGames, which is always concocting new tycoon adventures!

VISITED

FAVOURITED

CINDERING

POPULAR DEV EARNED HIS WINGS WITH SMASH-HIT SIMULATION GAMES

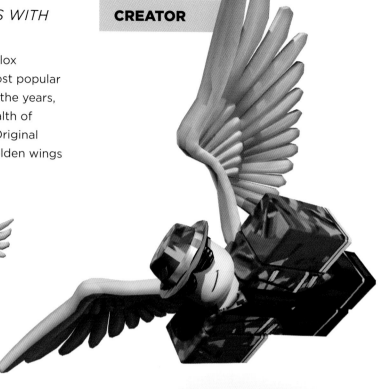

CREATOR

School's definitely 'in' for this Bloxy-winning Roblox developer, the headmaster of one of Roblox's most popular role-play experiences, Roblox High School. Over the years, Cindering's education RPG has earned him a wealth of glittering awards, including Best GUIs and Best Original Music Score, all of which go perfectly with his golden wings and blingin' style.

RED SPARKLE TIME FEDORA

GOLDEN SPARKLING WINGS

DEVELOPER TIMELINE

APRIL 2009
Cindering began his Roblox education with his role-play classic Roblox High School, which has hit over 2 million favourites from eager students and tired teachers.

AUGUST 2015
He released an update for Roblox High School, which added a whole host of brand new features, as well as an improved design for the school and map.

SEPTEMBER 2014
The hybrid tycoon game, Sharpshooter Mines, was released through his development group Cinder Studio. Players can mine with or snipe at other players.

FEBRUARY 2017
He won an astonishing five awards at the 4th annual Bloxys, including one for his Roblox High School: Fan Club group, which has over 3 million members.

CIRCUIT BREAKER

01101100 01101001 01110110 01100101 00100000 01110111 01101001 01110010 01100101

There's more to this apocalyptic android than just 1s and 0s! Circuit Breaker is a lean, mean, blox-busting machine and has an arsenal of weaponry to suit his destructive protocols. All Robloxians better watch out because he's one short circuit away from triggering his new subroutine ... total annihilation! Rules and circuits were meant to be broken!

CIRCUIT BREAKER'S HEAD

BLACK HOLE BOMB

ROBLOX FAMILY CHARACTER

LETTING OFF SOME STEAM IN ... PINEWOOD COMPUTER CORE

Being a technical trickster programmed to destroy the Robloxian race, it's no surprise that Circuit Breaker's favourite game is Pinewood Computer Core. At the underground complex, Circuit Breaker zooms around creating chaos, setting computers on fire and triggering malfunctions. His ultimate aim is to thwart the efforts of other players and initiate a complete core meltdown, destroying the facility entirely!

GAME STATS

DEVELOPER

Diddleshot

This sci-fi management game is one of Diddleshot's most popular creations. Diddleshot is also chairman of the Pinewood Builders group, which has over 83,000 devoted members!

VISITED

FAVOURITED

CLASSIC NOOB

EVER-PRESENT PLAYER WHO NEVER SEEMS TO GET ANY BETTER

They say our eyes are the window to our souls, and in the case of Classic Noob, it's clear to see his soul is made from sheer panic and bewilderment. This newcomer to the world of Roblox generally does more harm than good, but he's a handy team player, perfect for gunfight diversions, minefield clearing and basic cannon-fodder duties.

ROBLOX FAMILY CHARACTER

CLASSIC NOOB FACE

PROTEST SIGN: NOOBS

DOING WHAT HE DOES BEST IN ... CAR CRUSHERS 2

Classic Noob has tried his hand at every single classic Roblox game in a bid to find one game he's good at. Luckily, he stumbled across Car Crushers 2, where he gets rewarded for crashing, crushing and mashing cars, which he would've done anyway. He hasn't yet had the pleasure of causing an energy core meltdown, but it's only a matter of time before he obliterates the whole world ...

GAME STATS

DEVELOPER
Car Crushers Official Group

Car Crushers 2 is the second game in the series, building on the success of the original Car Crushers released by lead developer Panwellz. So far, the original has been visited over 22 million times!

VISITED

FAVOURITED

CLUB NYONIC: SINGER

SUPERSTAR SONGSTRESS BORN TO WOW SOLD-OUT CROWDS

Club Nyonic is home to a host of intriguing and charismatic Robloxians, but of all the visitors at the ultimate members' club, none are quite as glamorous or captivating as the butterfly-masked Club Nyonic: Singer. This digital diva loves nothing more than to belt out her number-one hits to a sold-out crowd of adoring super fans!

GAME CHARACTER

GLORIOUS PURPLE PARTY QUEEN

MICROPHONE

LIVE EVERY NIGHT AT 10PM IN ... CLUB NYONIC

GAME INFORMATION

Club Nyonic: Singer originates from the sprawling isle of Club Nyonic, a minigame-crammed getaway created by extravagant developer Nyonic! Players can fish for huge catches, send pins flying at the bowling alleys or ride a wave while out surfing. You can earn money, rent different items to play with and, if you're feeling flush with cash, you can even buy your own palatial home and live at Club Nyonic forever!

DEVELOPER
Nyonic

VISITED

FAVOURITED

DEFAULTIO
SCRIPTING SUPREMO WITH A BULGING TROPHY CABINET

To say Defaultio's supreme scripting and awesome developer skills are powered by his swanky Silverthorn Antlers and his dashingly Daring Beard would be, by default, an understatement. His true power lies within his unbridled imagination, which has helped him spawn a variety of tycoon-style games on Roblox, such as the evergreen Lumber Tycoon series!

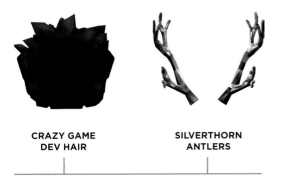

**CRAZY GAME
DEV HAIR**

**SILVERTHORN
ANTLERS**

CREATOR

DEVELOPER TIMELINE

OCTOBER 2008
Immediately after signing up to Roblox, Defaultio started work on his first wood-harvesting tycoon game, Lumber Tycoon, which proved extremely popular.

DECEMBER 2011
Defaultio's Belmont Mountain was chosen to host an event for the 2011 Roblox Present Giveaway, where players had to find badges to trade for gifts.

JULY 2009
Less than a year after the original first hit the front page, Defaultio moved his focus onto a sequel and began work on smash-hit Lumber Tycoon 2.

QUICK FACT
Defaultio has won loads of awards, including a BLOXcon 2014 Golden Scroll, RDC 2017 and 2016 Game Jam trophies, and two 2016 Bloxy Awards.

DIGGIN ALL DOGS

CANINE CONNOISSEUR AND DEVOTED COMPANION TO MAN'S BEST FRIEND

Is it the canine snacks she has in her pooch-pouch, or her uncanny skill of whistling at just the right doggy frequency that makes her so pup-ular? Whatever it is, Diggin All Dogs is the leader of the pack! She is truly the best buddy of man's best friend and has a canine style that gets everyone's tails wagging!

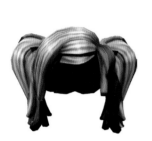

HONEY BLONDE PONYTAIL

ATTACK DOGE

ROBLOX FAMILY CHARACTER

CHASING AFTER HER CANINE PALS IN ... WOLVES' LIFE 2

Though she prefers to spend her time with her canine pals, Diggin All Dogs has found herself addicted to the lupine role-play classic Wolves' Life 2. She's the alpha wolf in her own pack, which she's christened Waggin All Wolves. She loves leading her wolfpack on epic adventures throughout the wide open world, as well as chilling with her pack at her cosy den near the wild Wet Fur Waterpark.

GAME STATS

DEVELOPER
Shyfoox Studios

This barkingly brilliant game was created by Shyfoox Studios, an animal role-play group with over 305,000 members, owned by developer and confirmed animal lover Shyfoox.

VISITED

FAVOURITED

DIZZYPURPLE

LOOKS CAN BE DECEIVING FOR THIS UNLIKELY STYLE SAVANT

Yep, that's a traffic cone hat on his head, but don't let DizzyPurple's unique fashion sense fool you. This style icon developer knows what it takes to win a catwalk-battle in Top Roblox Runway Model. After gaining over 100 million visits since 2014, Top Roblox Runway Model is DizzyPurple's most popular Roblox creation to date.

CREATOR

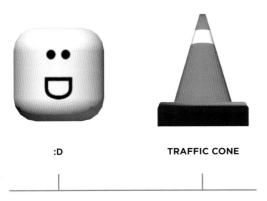

:D   TRAFFIC CONE

DEVELOPER TIMELINE

JUNE 2014
He began tailoring the stylish dress-up-challenge game Roblox Top Model, where players hit the catwalk to win the approval of the design-eyed judges.

AUGUST 2017
DizzyPurple rebranded the fashion smash-hit Roblox Top Model to Top Roblox Runway Model, during an update that improved the fashion formula further still.

JANUARY 2015
DizzyPurple's fashion super hit, Roblox Top Model, was chosen to be part of the Roblox Winter Games event, with two special event hats to be won.

QUICK FACT
He has over 140 million place visits and more than 30,000 followers.

DOLLASTICDREAMS

*YOUTUBE SENSATION WITH A
FONDNESS FOR ROLE-PLAY GAMES*

DollasticDreams is a Roblox super fan, family-friendly gamer, YouTube sensation and colossal collector of all things cute! If there ever existed a gigantic pool filled with the world's fluffiest stuffed animals and toys, she'd be the first to dive in ... head first. You can track down this Roblox celebrity playing her all-time fave games MeepCity and Roblox High School!

**BANDLEADER
GUINEA PIG FRIEND**

BLACK AND RED

INFLUENCER

COMMUNITY STATS

**YOUTUBE
CHANNEL**
DOLLASTIC PLAYS!

**MOST POPULAR
VIDEO**
Roblox Neverland
Mermaid Lagoon –
Adventure of Ursulo &
Lariel – with Gamer Chad

VIEWS

SUBSCRIBERS

**ROBLOX
FOLLOWERS**

116k+

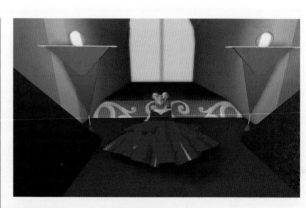

MEMORABLE MOMENT
DollasticDreams enrolled at the magical Royale High, donned a beautiful red dress and then ... skipped all her classes! However, she spent her time customising her awesome dorm room. Luckily she had her royal card to account for her wild expenditures, including an adorable set of Lovely Bunk Beds for when her friends come to stay.

DORM LIFE: PEER COUNSELLOR

APPROACHABLE STAFFER WITH AN EAR TO LEND AND A SHOULDER TO CRY ON

Every day is a lazy day for the laid-back Dorm Life: Peer Counsellor. She and her uber-friendly pooch will always lend an ear or two to any Robloxian who knocks on their always-open door. Her long-winded marathon lectures may sound exhausting, but she always imparts priceless Dorm Life advice.

ROBLOX FAMILY CHARACTER

NERD GLASSES

HULA DOG

DISPENSING WISDOM IN ... ROYALE HIGH

Dorm Life: Peer Counsellor isn't at home if she isn't helping somebody, so in her spare time she likes to ply her trade in one of her favourite Roblox games, Royale High. Residents of the enchanting high school can take classes in everything from baking and dance to chemistry and English. But if one of the students ever has an issue, they can fly right over to the Counsellor, who will solve any problems.

GAME STATS

DEVELOPER
callmehbob

The creator of Royale High is callmehbob, a seasoned developer who is also responsible for other magical game experiences such as Fantasia Getaway Resort Hotel and Autumn Town.

VISITED

FAVOURITED

DUED1

VIRTUOSO DEVELOPER SEEMINGLY ABLE TO EXCEL IN ANY GENRE

Who doesn't like a hot and delicious pizza straight out of the oven? Pizza-loving developer Dued1 certainly does, and he has indulged his culinary desires by creating the classic Roblox food-sim Work at a Pizza Place. Since he joined Roblox in 2007, Dued1 has attracted a massive fan base thanks to his hit game and his love of a perfectly prepared pizza!

CREATOR

BEAUTIFUL HAIR FOR BEAUTIFUL PEOPLE

8-BALL HEADPHONES

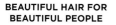

DEVELOPER TIMELINE

MARCH 2008
After six months of finding his feet on Roblox, Dued1 started to develop the game that would eventually become simulation hit Work at a Pizza Place.

APRIL 2015
This talented developer tried his hand at a new challenge and started to create Maze Journey, which contained randomly generated labyrinths.

AUGUST 2009
Dued1 decided to take on a different type of project next, and within three hours he had built the framework of long-range combat game Sniper City.

NOVEMBER 2015
Work at a Pizza Place received an update so that it can be played on the go with its new mobile-friendly version. You'll never miss an order now!

EPIC MINER

WHISTLING WHILE HE WORKS, WITH A PICKAXE IN HAND AND A SMILE ON HIS FACE

Having fulfilled his life-long dream of becoming a master excavator, Epic Miner now journeys around Robloxia in his customised mine-cart, sniffing out the world's most extraordinary gems. Armed with nothing but his trusted pickaxe, iconic hardhat and a deep desire to dig, Epic Miner has a subterranean determination to mine like he's never mined before!

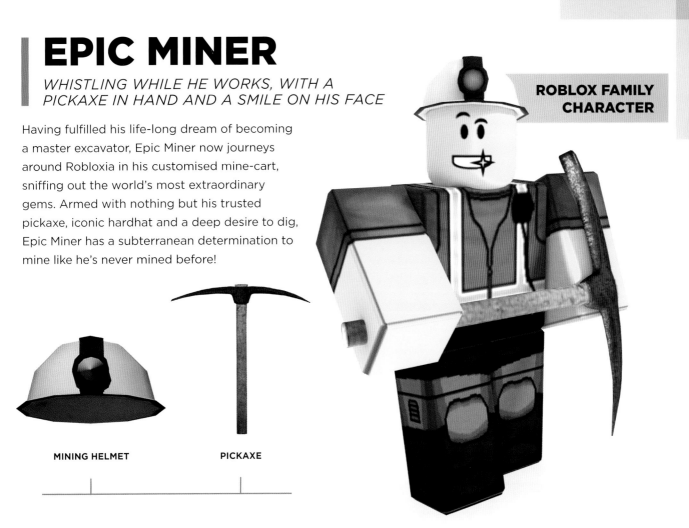

MINING HELMET   PICKAXE

DRILLING FOR RARE ORES IN ... MINING INC!

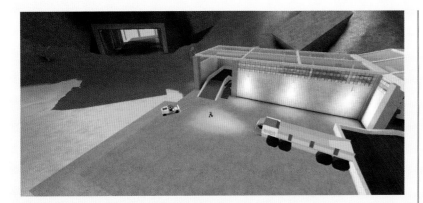

He was born, trained and moulded to mine, so in between his everyday drilling, extracting and refining, Epic Miner loves to educate other would-be miners and play the co-op mining sim Mining INC!. He is an integral part of any playful mining endeavour and doesn't mind helping out wherever he's needed – drilling, extracting or refining raw minerals – making his team a quarry load of money in the process!

GAME STATS

DEVELOPER
Widgeon

This team-based mining game has excavated over 120,000 favourites and is the most popular game of developer Widgeon's impressive portfolio, which also includes The Plaza and Aegis.

VISITED

FAVOURITED

ERIK.CASSEL

MUCH BELOVED FOUNDING MEMBER OF ROBLOX, WHOSE LEGACY LIVES ON

As one of the proud founding members of Roblox alongside Builderman, Erik.Cassel was known for being relentlessly supportive and an inspiration to all who knew him. He was a true engineer at heart and a devoted friend and masterful mentor. Erik.Cassel's legacy lives on at the heart of the Roblox ethos and he will fondly and forever be remembered.

ROBLOX CLASSIC

ERIK.CASSEL'S HAT

CLASSIC ROBLOXIAN FACE

ONE OF HIS FAVOURITE GAMES WAS ... CROSSROADS

An enthusiastic devotee to all things Roblox, Erik always encouraged boundaries to be pushed, and one of his favourite games did just that. The brick-battle arena Crossroads was created by the team at Roblox, and was the first multiplayer game on the platform. Players enter a map filled with towers, bridges, caves and hideouts, and battle it out in the free-for-all world armed with rocket launchers, swords, bombs and a handy wall-building trowel.

GAME STATS

DEVELOPER
Roblox

Crossroads is one of the oldest and most recognised places on Roblox and was created by some of the early team members at Roblox including David Baszucki, Erik Cassel and John Shedletsky.

VISITED

FAVOURITED

EVILARTIST

CREATIVE COMMUNITY MEMBER WITH A USERNAME THAT'S ONLY HALF TRUE

EvilArtist is her name, drawing is her game! Since joining the Roblox community, EvilArtist has been honing her sketching skills by creating portraits of other players' avatars, as well as illustrating all kinds of beautiful masterpieces for the community. As a 2016 Bloxy Award nominee, her positivity and boundless imagination are an inspiration to Roblox artists all over the world.

CREATOR

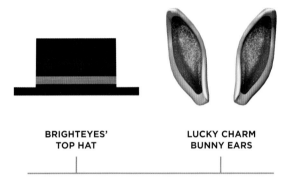

BRIGHTEYES' TOP HAT

LUCKY CHARM BUNNY EARS

DEVELOPER FACTS

This game-playing artist discovered the creative medium of Roblox and joined the party in July 2012.

ROBLOX

JUL 2012

EvilArtist is a freelance illustrator and loves to sketch everything and anything that is Roblox.

She was commissioned to design and illustrate the new group logo for the investing group Trade.

She runs a social fan club group called the Vivinions which has over 450 art-loving members.

This freelance sketcher has also drawn logos for the game development group From The Deep.

EZEBEL: THE PIRATE QUEEN

FEARLESS LEADER OF HER OWN
MERRY BAND OF PIRATES

After graduating top of her class, Ezebel could have been anything she wanted – the world was her oyster. So, logically she became a pirate! Everything Ezebel learned in school has come in handy since she set sail into the swashbuckling world of rapscallions and buccaneers, and she has risen through the seafaring ranks to become a grade-A Queen of the high seas!

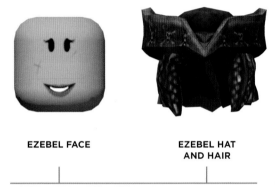

EZEBEL FACE

EZEBEL HAT AND HAIR

ROBLOX FAMILY CHARACTER

LEADING A RESCUE OPERATION IN ... ROBLOX TITANIC

As seafaring royalty herself, Ezebel is drawn to games with an ocean view, and her current favourite experience is the role-play classic Roblox Titanic. With her crew of friends, Ezebel loves recreating the dramatic events of the Titanic's catastrophic maiden voyage over one hundred years ago, and tries to rewrite history by heroically attempting to save passengers from the icy depths.

GAME STATS

DEVELOPER
Virtual Valley Games

This beautifully modelled historical game by Virtual Valley Games has dramatic role-play elements that have made it a popular Roblox experience, earning over 19 million visits since release.

VISITED

FAVOURITED

FIREBRAND1

ROBLOXIAN CITY BUILDER AND PREVALENT COMMUNITY LEADER

A source of pure imagination, Firebrand1 is one of the earliest Robloxian pioneers. His crowning glory is not his legendary Purple Ice Crown, but the smash-hit game RoCitizens, which allows you to role-play at life ... find a job, buy a house and hang out with friendly Robloxians. The perfect escape from your real-life tasks, like finding a job, buying a house and hanging out with your friends ...

PURPLE ICE CROWN

SPECTOLOUPES

CREATOR

DEVELOPER TIMELINE

FEBRUARY 2009
This avid gamer and soon-to-be master developer stoked the fires of his imagination and joined the Roblox community in the early days of 2009.

ROBLOX

FEB 2009

FEBRUARY 2017
Firebrand1 was one of the stars returning from the 4th Annual Bloxy Awards with a trophy, claiming the grand prize for Most Concurrent Users on PC.

DECEMBER 2013
He started to forge the place that would eventually become his hit classic RoCitizens, which has attracted over 200 million visits to date.

QUICK FACT
Firebrand1 runs the fan club RoCitizens Community, which has over 150,000 passionate role-play fans.

FRAMED: SPY

CLUMSY, DISTANT AND HOPELESS – THAT'S JUST WHAT SHE WANTS YOU TO THINK

In the stealthy, high-action Roblox thriller Framed!, everyone is a possible enemy, so don't be fooled by Framed: Spy's aloof nature: she is the ultimate femme fatale. She might brazenly declare her life as an undercover operative on her hat, but she only speaks one language – deception. So those who believe her lies better watch their backs!

GAME CHARACTER

OBVIOUS SPY CAP

BULL MOOSE PARTY

HUNTING NOOBS IN ... FRAMED!

GAME INFORMATION

The deadly Spy is from the Roblox thriller game Framed! by developer pa00. Players must locate and stealthily kill their target, while keeping an eye out for trigger-happy undercover cops in this espionage thriller! Every hunter is also hunted, as other spies try to track down their own targets. With a range of fun murder-mystery maps, Framed! has had more than 27 million visits from secret-agents to date.

DEVELOPER
pa00

VISITED

FAVOURITED

FUZZYWOOO

MONOCHROMATIC MAIDEN WHO IS AN EXPERT AT CREATING SEA-BASED SCARES

The true jack-of-all-trades, developer FuzzyWooo has lent her skilful hand to building and scripting games, as well as crafting a stylish selection of clothes. Most people will know this multi-faceted maker as the creator of the jaw-snapping Shark Attack!, but she has also dabbled in Robloxian role-play experiences and embarked on a new venture back into the shark-infested sea.

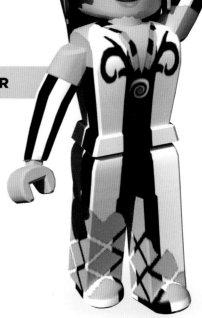

CREATOR

MONOCHROME LIBRARY HAIR

ELF EARS

DEVELOPER TIMELINE

OCTOBER 2015
FuzzyWooo started a new development adventure and began work on her monster hit Shark Attack!, which has welcomed over 11 million visitors to its deadly waters.

QUICK FACT
She has her very own badge that is awarded every time a gamer happens to meet her in Shark Attack!

OCTOBER 2017
Two years after the epic success of her first game, this shark-hunting developer began work on a sequel to Shark Attack, subtitled Shark Battle!

QUICK FACT
FuzzyWooo created the Roblox community group Shark Attack Fan Club, which has a membership of over 3,500.

GALAXY GIRL

PLANET-HOPPING ROBLOXIAN WITH A PERSONALITY THAT'S OUT OF THIS WORLD

Rocking through the cosmos and dancing between the stars, it's the interstellar Galaxy Girl. This intergalactic adventurer was the first to be born in outer space. As she explores the great unknown, she holds on to her cosmic dream that one day she will reach the final frontier, Earth, and meet the great human race!

PURPLE GALAXY GAZE

ULTRAVIOLET BLASTER

FLEET COMMANDER IN ... GALAXY

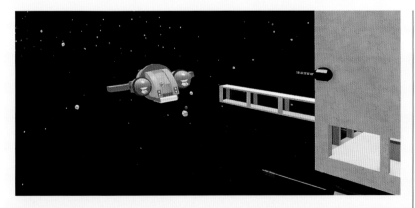

Having originated from the ether of the cosmos, Galaxy Girl can't get enough of sci-fi game Galaxy. She has her own faction, Girls of the Galaxy, and commands a flotilla of space-faring ships of all sizes. Galaxy Girl doesn't hide behind her comrades, she leads from the front – mining, trading, and crafting bigger and better ships – so she can win the battle for the stars!

GAME STATS

DEVELOPER
rcouret

This elite sandbox space game is one of developer rcouret's epic adventure creations on Roblox, following his previous entry, the medieval conquest simulation Field of Battle.

VISITED

FAVOURITED

GEEGEE92

ADORED FOR HER FRIENDLY PERSONALITY AND HER FUNNY VIDEOS

The community celebrity Geegee92 (AKA SallyGreenGamer on YouTube) is a famous, family-friendly gamer who likes playing Roblox with her daughters. She loves the wide mix of awesome games on Roblox and the huge imagination that goes into making them. Her absolute must-play games include the ever-popular MeepCity and Roblox Deathrun.

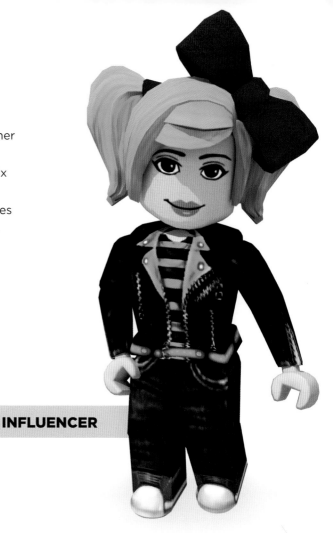

HONEY FACE

GREEN HAIR WITH OVERSIZED BOW

INFLUENCER

COMMUNITY STATS

YOUTUBE CHANNEL

SallyGreenGamer

MOST POPULAR VIDEO

Roblox Freeze Tag with Audrey

VIEWS

SUBSCRIBERS

ROBLOX FOLLOWERS

67k+

MEMORABLE MOMENT

GeeGee92 dropped into the stylist sim Fashion Famous to teach her fellow contestants a thing or two about how to work the catwalk. One of the rounds tasked players with dressing up as a character from a story book, and GeeGee chose this opportunity to dress up as ... Santa Claus. Her outfit was judged to be second best, as she just lost out to another Santa Claus! What are the odds?

GIANT HUNTER

PERSONAL PHILOSOPHY: THE BIGGER THEY ARE, THE HARDER THEY FALL

It's no small task being a hunter of Robloxia's largest brutes! Giant Hunter has honed her skills in the art of giant-slaying and toppled many a mammoth monster in the hugely popular Giant Survival. The secret to her gigantic success is teamwork – the more the merrier on the hunt – and if all else fails and the giant prevails, she's excellent at hiding too!

GAME CHARACTER

CROSSBOW

NOT SURE IF...

TROPHY HUNTING IN ... GIANT SURVIVAL

GAME INFORMATION

This character is native to the hugely popular Giant Survival, which has welcomed over 50 million giant-hunters. Players are teleported into a small map full of buildings that an enormous giant wants to destroy. The team attempt to take down the marauding giant without being squished or flattened by the huge foe or falling debris. There's an array of weapons, as well as a range of giants to combat, including a gigantic ghost!

DEVELOPER
BuildIntoGames

VISITED

FAVOURITED

GIRL GUEST

NEWBIE GAMER LOOKING FOR FUN, FRIENDS AND ADVENTURES

Meet the new girl on the blox! Girl Guest may come across a little shy at first, but once you get to know her, you'll have a Roblox friend for life. She's always down to play games, especially Hide & Seek, and once you've found her again, she'd love to hang out and go on lots of brand-new adventures with her new BFF.

ROBLOX FAMILY CHARACTER

PINKTASTIC HAIR

CLASSIC ROBLOXIAN HEAD

ESCAPING TO NEW DIMENSIONS IN ... THE NORMAL ELEVATOR

This newcomer to the world of Roblox wanted to start with a normal experience, in a normal game ... so she chose The Normal Elevator! She certainly wasn't expecting what she got, but she's been riding it with her new best friends ever since – dodging dinosaurs, fleeing runaway trains and sheltering from a storm of sharks. She can't wait to see what she finds on the next floor!

GAME STATS

DEVELOPER
NowDoTheHarlemShake

This award-winning adventure game by NowDoTheHarlemShake has had over 190 million visits to its eclectic world of minigames. For more absurdist gaming, try his other hit, The Normal City.

VISITED

FAVOURITED

GUSMANAK

PROLIFIC CREATOR WITH AN UNBELIEVABLE GAMUT OF GAMES

Resplendent in his golden attire and adorned with the legendary Dominus Aureus, Gusmanak is one of Roblox's elite creators. This renowned developer and founder of development studio Dualpoint Interactive was awarded Game Developer of the Year in 2013, and is most recognised for creating the Roblox classics Apocalypse Rising and Tiny Tanks.

DOMINUS AUREUS

GAME TRAILER VIDEO CONTEST WINNER

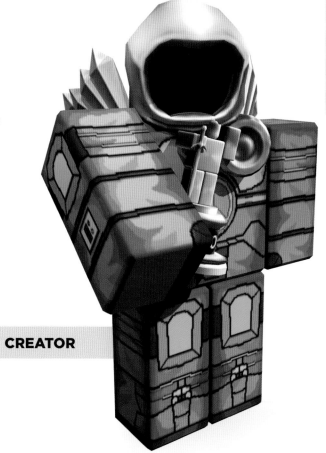

CREATOR

DEVELOPER TIMELINE

APRIL 2008
After joining Roblox on April Fools' Day, Gusmanak set to work creating the world for his outrageously popular Apocalypse Rising, proving he was no joke.

JANUARY 2015
Gusmanak helped launch the vehicular battle game Tiny Tanks with NWSpacek and Sharksie. It was one of the first Roblox games available on Xbox One.

JULY 2013
Several years after its inception, Apocalypse Rising earned Gusmanak two awards at the transatlantic BLOXcon events held in Chicago and London.

JUNE 2017
The much-awaited sequel to his phenomenal survival hit, Apocalypse Rising 2 started to take shape. Such was the demand that an alpha version was released.

HAGGIE125

SKILLED DEV DEDICATED TO PUSHING THE BOUNDARIES OF ROBLOX GAMES

A talented and enchanting developer, Haggie125 has harnessed the ancient power of the cubic void to construct a far-reaching portfolio of popular games that includes Retail Tycoon, Morbus, Solar Scuffle and many, many more. He is also the owner of Secondhand Studios, a group dedicated to crafting even more immersive user-generated experiences on Roblox.

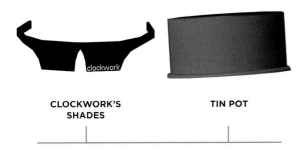

CLOCKWORK'S SHADES

TIN POT

CREATOR

DEVELOPER TIMELINE

JULY 2008
After a few months getting himself familiar with the world of Roblox, Haggie125 started work on Ice Hockey, which over 340,000 sports fans have played.

MAY 2014
Having covered sports and simulation, six years into his Roblox adventure, Haggie125 added an entry to a new genre and released the infectious Morbus.

JUNE 2013
Haggie125 showcased his ever-expanding skillset by launching his most expansive project, Medievalville, an open world game with many facets.

AUGUST 2015
The prolific developer began work on his most successful game to date, Retail Tycoon, which has attracted over 100 million visits since release.

HANG GLIDER

*SHE'S LOOKING FOR THRILLS WITH
HER HEAD FIRMLY IN THE CLOUDS*

This high-flying Robloxian was born and raised in the
windswept bloxy valleys of Chaos Canyon. Hang Glider
now pursues a bold lifestyle gliding among the clouds of
Robloxia, keeping a watchful eye over the world below.
She always has her eyes open for her next big
adventure and is ready to swoop down
and save the day.

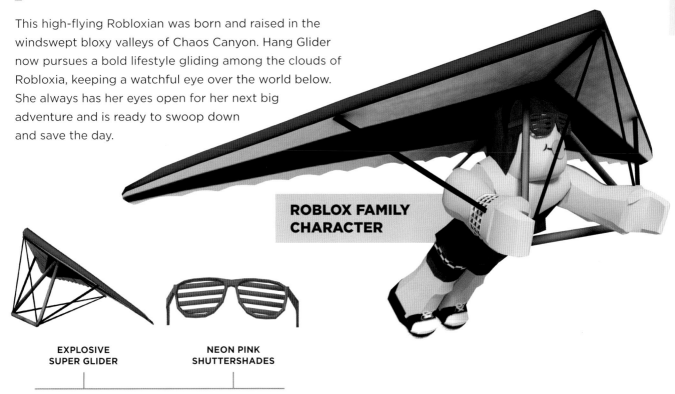

**ROBLOX FAMILY
CHARACTER**

**EXPLOSIVE
SUPER GLIDER**

**NEON PINK
SHUTTERSHADES**

SOARING OVERHEAD IN ... THE PLAZA

Hang Glider's action-packed lifestyle can begin to take its toll after a
while, so she likes to relax down at The Plaza. She can kick back at her
own apartment, or take a leisurely stroll around town to meet the other
citizens and see the sights.

GAME STATS

DEVELOPER
Widgeon

The Plaza is Widgeon's most
popular game to date, attracting
around 100 million visitors since it
was released. He recently released
a new game, Aegis, in beta on the
Roblox platform.

VISITED

FAVOURITED

HIGH SCHOOL DUDE

HE'S TOO COOL FOR SCHOOL, BUT HIS MOM MAKES HIM GO ANYWAY

He may look mysteriously stoic on the outside, but don't let his dark, brooding demeanor fool you; High School Dude has a sabre-like, sarcastic wit and charmingly dry sense of humor. You can spot this angst-fuelled dude cruising around Roblox High School on his skateboard as he tries to get to class on time.

CRIMSON SHADES

CRIMSON WINTER SCARF

HANDSOMELY BROODING IN ... SHARPSHOOTER MINES

GAME INFORMATION

When he's not hanging out under the bleachers of Cindering's role-play classic Roblox High School, he's at home playing competitive building game Sharpshooter Mines, created by Cindering's Cinder Studio. High School Dude loves mining ore by day to power his factory, building cool stuff and crafting weapons, then by night he heads out into the mine arena looking to engage in a little miner-on-miner sharpshooting.

DEVELOPER

Cinder Studio

VISITED

FAVOURITED

HIGH SCHOOL GAL

THE MOST POPULAR GIRL IN SCHOOL WHO SETS ALL THE TRENDS

She's the queen of the classroom, blessed with brains and a chic fashion sense that dictates the style of the school. High School Gal is a natural leader and with her textbook-carrying friends in tow, she's ready to achieve top grades and show everyone how to be the perfect student!

GAME CHARACTER

LEI

PINK SPARKLE TIME FEDORA

DOING DOUGHNUTS IN THE PARKING LOT OF ... ROBLOX HIGH SCHOOL

GAME INFORMATION

High School Gal also hails from the massively popular Roblox High School by Cindering. The high school classic has had over 480 million enrollments since its doors opened in 2009. In the game, players can choose between a role as the school's principal, one of the teaching staff, or a student. Players can check out the timetable and get to class on time, then hang out at the skate park when the school day ends.

DEVELOPER
Cindering (p. 28)

VISITED

FAVOURITED

HUNTED VAMPIRE

TERROR OF THE COLD, DARK NIGHT, RESIGNED TO HIDING IN SHADOWS

Legend has it that once, when the world of Robloxia was covered in shadows, an ancient vampire terrorised the land. This primordial presence preyed in the darkness and sucked the life from the living, until a legendary detective cast a shaft of heroic light into the gloom. Now the ancient fiend is reduced to cowering in the shadows and is known as the Hunted Vampire.

GAME CHARACTER

MOSTLY GHOSTLY POTION

SPINE-CHILLING SWORD

LURKING SOMEWHERE IN ... VAMPIRE HUNTERS 2

GAME INFORMATION

The fanged Hunted Vampire skulks in the shadows of the atmospheric Vampire Hunters 2. Gamers get to customise their character before entering the shadowy world of vamps. Players are split into teams of vampires, humans and detectives. Vampires lurk in the darkness looking to feast on the living, while gun-toting detectives try to track down the undead fiends, and humans just try to survive until the end of the round.

DEVELOPER
ZacAttackk

VISITED

FAVOURITED

INITIATE OF GLORIOUS FLIGHT

A GODLY MAGE WHO WIELDS COMPASSION, KINDNESS AND AN AWESOME SCEPTRE

ROBLOX FAMILY CHARACTER

A young, idealistic mage, Initiate of Glorious Flight devotes her life to the sacred scriptures so she will one day perfect her wondrous craft. Her affluent robes may give her an air of higher-being, which is quite literally the case due to her dominion over air and space, but Initiate of Glorious Flight is also humble and uses her powers to protect all bloxkind.

INITIATE OF GLORIOUS FLIGHT MAGIC STAFF

INITIATE OF GLORIOUS FLIGHT HAIR

PURSUING ENLIGHTENMENT IN ... TEMPLE OF MEMORIES

After years of contemplation and peaceful scholarship, the Initiate of Glorious Flight has excelled in learning the power of thoughtful calm. Her most-visited spot for tranquility – a necessity for practising her zen-like aura – is in a beautifully crafted showcase, Temple of Memories. She can lose herself in hours of quiet exploration atop snowy peaks or windy valleys ... or simply stand still to grow her sense of enlightenment.

GAME STATS

DEVELOPER

Crykee

This expertly fashioned world of Far East architecture comes from the imagination of visual artist Crykee. He also works on games with Biostream, releasing them through their studio, Bitsquid Games.

VISITED

FAVOURITED

INMATE

THIS CAGED ANIMAL HAS A CUNNING PLAN TO BREAK LOOSE

He did the crime and now he's doing the time. However, Inmate has had enough of his hard-knock life behind bars in the classic role-play game Prison Life, and longs to see the great wide world of Robloxia once more. He's a con man with a plan, and he is masterminding the perfect escape, but first he needs to distract the gullible guards!

ERR...   BROWN HAIR DUDE

DOING HARD TIME IN ... PRISON LIFE

GAME INFORMATION
Based on Aesthetical's action classic Prison Life, the Inmate has chosen a life behind bars. Players can follow in his footsteps, attempt to escape imprisonment and help others to freedom. First inmates must avoid the guards and try to get their criminal hands on useful items like keycards and hammers. Then they must use stealth or brute force to escape, with the odd gun coming in handy when making the dash for freedom.

DEVELOPER
Aesthetical (p. 7)

VISITED

FAVOURITED

JULIE

INTENT ON RULING THE WORLD, SHE WON'T LET ANYTHING STAND IN HER WAY

She's just a girl who's looking for a friend to help her execute her lifelong dream ... world domination! Don't let her sweet smile make you think she's kind and caring – she's quite the opposite, and she has an inner steel that is focused on surviving and dominating loleris' iconic Roblox experience, Mad Games.

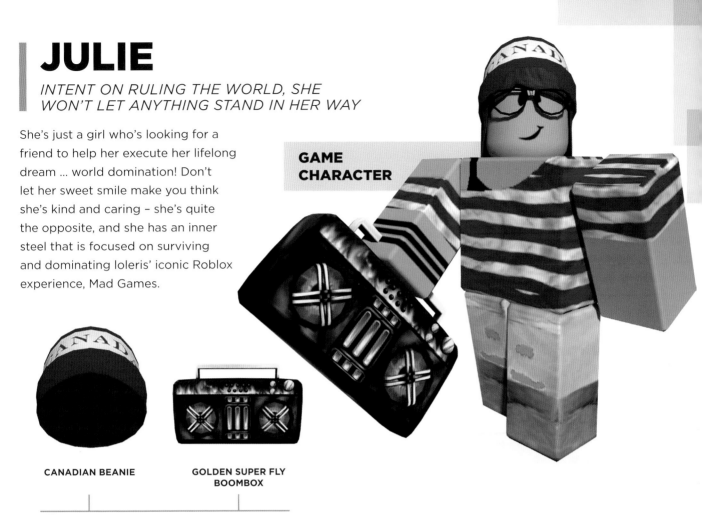

GAME CHARACTER

CANADIAN BEANIE

GOLDEN SUPER FLY BOOMBOX

SNIPING NOOBS IN ... MAD PAINTBALL 2

Taking some time away from work is important to Julie; world domination doesn't happen overnight, after all. To relax she spends hours on one of her favourite games, Mad Paintball 2. After arming herself with an arsenal of colour-slinging weapons, she jumps into a game and splats her enemies without mercy.

GAME STATS

DEVELOPER
loleris (p. 69)

The brains behind the 'Mad' franchise of games is loleris. Other releases in the series include Mad Wars 2 and The Mad Murderer, which has been favourited over 345,000 times.

VISITED

FAVOURITED

KEITH

LYNCHPIN OF THE ROBLOX COMMUNITY AND A TRUSTED RIGHT-HAND MAN

Keith has known Builderman for years and together they have formed a partnership that helps fuel the imagination of people all around the world. Keith is a huge advocate of scalability and works hard to promote a robust social network of Robloxian creators and builders. If you're very lucky, you may catch him playing his favourite game, Prison Life, in his spare time.

ROBLOX CLASSIC

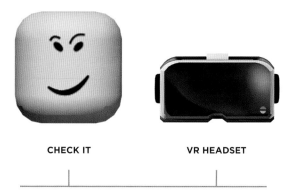

CHECK IT   VR HEADSET

ONE OF HIS FAVOURITE GAMES IS ... PRISON LIFE

ROBLOXIA PRISON

Enjoy your stay!

Upon escaping from Roblox HQ for another day, Keith loves to spend his spare time playing cops and robbers in Prison Life. Being an upstanding member of society, Keith opts to assume the role of prison guard and does his best to maintain order in the chaotic prison. If an inmate is lucky enough to make it out of jail on his watch, you can be sure that Keith will be the first to hop in a chopper to hunt them down.

GAME STATS

DEVELOPER
Aesthetical (p. 7)

This prison-break simulation comes from the imagination of award-winning creator Aesthetical. Prison Life was awarded a Bloxy in 2017 for the most visitors, as well as one for most visitors on mobile!

VISITED

FAVOURITED

KORBLOX DEATHSPEAKER

TALKS ABOUT HIS FELLOW KORBLOXIANS BEHIND THEIR BACKS

Don't listen to what others say about this hideous fiend – Korblox Deathspeaker is pure and uncontrolled evil who strikes terror in his foes. Any villain who wears spiky armour with such devilish ease is bound to be up to no good, so you better watch out for this bad guy's evil antics, especially when he has his Korblox Mage Staff pointed at you!

**KORBLOX
DEATHSPEAKER HOOD**

**KORBLOX
MAGE STAFF**

**ROBLOX FAMILY
CHARACTER**

SETTING DEVIOUS TRAPS IN ... DEATHRUN

Korblox Deathspeaker talks a good game and, as it happens, he runs one too, in his all-time favourite game Roblox Deathrun. As the killer, he loves activating the traps and blowing up the runners. He also enjoys the odd game as a runner, defying the devices of death, so he can reach the finish and use his sword to clinch victory!

GAME STATS

DEVELOPER
Team Deathrun

This devilishly addictive survival game has run up over 105 million visits, hosted seasonal Roblox events, and earned lead developer Wsly and Team Deathrun several Bloxy Awards.

VISITED

FAVOURITED

KORBLOX GENERAL

SUPREME COMMANDER OF THE ENTIRE KORBLOXIAN MILITARY MIGHT

In the ever-lasting fight for the kingdom of Robloxia, the evil Korbloxian armies are commanded by the master warrior Korblox General. He has studied the great war tacticians and strategists from history, mastered the ancient techniques of combat, and, in extreme circumstances, he can shout really loudly to make his army charge with a frenzied fury.

KORBLOX SWORD AND SHIELD

KORBLOX GENERAL

COMMANDING AN ARMY IN ... AFTER THE FLASH: DEEP SIX

Korblox General loves being in charge, so when not on the front lines of the Korblox-Redcliff war, he's commanding a squad of survivors in After The Flash: Deep Six. He enjoys customising his player with a cool name, complex backstory and apocalyptic outfit before joining a faction, taking charge and roaming the atmospheric map. When enemies encounter the General, they'll wish that they hadn't survived the 'Flash' after all ...

GAME STATS

DEVELOPER

ChadTheCreator

After The Flash: Deep Six is the sixth installment in the ambitious role-play saga by After The Flash Advisory Board, a role-play group created by ChadTheCreator, who's also famous for Club Boates.

VISITED

FAVOURITED

KORBLOX MAGE

DIABOLICAL SPELL-SLINGING SHAMAN OF THE KORBLOX MILITARY FORCE

A dark, menacing magic pulses through this nihilistic necromancer's vile veins, giving him the power to cast destruction in his wake. Sporting a horned helmet and clad in the finest armour, Korblox Mage is spell-bent on using his devastating black magic to assist the Korbloxian army's cause and help them to conquer all of Robloxia.

ROBLOX FAMILY CHARACTER

BLIZZARD BEAST MODE

KORBLOX BONE MACE

OBLITERATING THE RUNNERS IN ... ARCHMAGE

The Korblox have a taste for an addictive run-and-survive-style game, and Korblox Mage is no different. His favourite Roblox game is the magical Archmage, where he gets to show off his sorcery skills, and rain spells down on runners as they try to complete the astral assault course and dethrone him from the Archmage's castle.

GAME STATS

DEVELOPER
Negative Games

This open-world creation by Negative Games, led by inventive developer Imaginaerum, cast its spell over one million visitors in the first three months after its release in summer 2017.

VISITED

FAVOURITED

LANDO64000

TALENTED DEVELOPER FAMOUS FOR EXPANSIVE EXPERIENCES

Dressed in his dapper steampunk style, lando64000 is a true Robloxian gentleman at heart and is a gifted developer with a penchant for cleverly-disguised secret areas. Some of this suave creator's finest games include the classic Hide and Seek, with its forty-one maps to explore, and the swashbuckling Roblox adventure game A Pirate's Life.

GENTLEMAN'S LAPEL FLOWER

BRIGHTEYED STEAMPUNK

CREATOR

DEVELOPER TIMELINE

MARCH 2009
lando64000 weighed anchor on a new idea and began his voyage into game creation with the swashbuckling adventure game A Pirate's Life.

APRIL 2015
After the success of his first Hide and Seek title, lando64000 began crafting a remastered version, appropriately named Hide and Seek Remastered.

APRIL 2009
The debonair creator hid himself away and started work on the original version of his Hide and Seek game, which has found over 18 million visitors.

QUICK FACT
At the 4th Annual Bloxy Awards, lando64000 took home the award for Game of the Year.

LET'S MAKE A DEAL

EVERYTHING HAS A PRICE, BUT HE WON'T PAY MORE THAN HALF

He's got everything that you need, but it comes at a price! Let's Make a Deal is the definitive salesman – he won't let you walk away without an armful of purchases! With his trademark brown LMaD suit and flashy multicoloured hairstyle, this epic entrepreneur knows the dark art of the deal and is always on the lookout for a bargain!

ROBLOX FAMILY CHARACTER

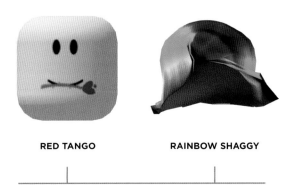

RED TANGO

RAINBOW SHAGGY

DOING BUSINESS IN ... MOON TYCOON

After a day of wheeling and dealing, Let's Make a Deal loves putting on his moon boots and reaching for the stars. He's always dreamed of owning the galaxy, and in Moon Tycoon he can do just that, with a little moon mining, spaceship flying and laser-gun negotiating thrown in for an all-around intergalactic gaming experience!

GAME STATS

DEVELOPER
Lethal682

Moon Tycoon was developer Lethal682's first foray into the tycoon genre and it notched him over 35 million cosmic visits, and that number is rocketing with every passing day!

VISITED

FAVOURITED

LILLY_S

*COMMUNITY PARAGON AND
INSPIRATION FOR ENTIRE BATTALIONS*

Lilly_S is the benevolent empress of the planet Kytheriia and the high-priestess of the Roblox developers' relations team. She commands an army of over 160,000 people, and her fearsome group was nominated in 2017 for the Best Battle Group Bloxy Award. Join Lilly_S's ranks for a fun campaign of excitement, but be sure to stay in Her Majesty's good graces!

**LADY OF THE
FEDERATION**

GOLDEN HAIR

CREATOR

DEVELOPER TIMELINE

EARLY 2011
After a year playing around on Roblox, Lilly_S spawned into Vortex Security's Recruiting Center and joined the ranks of the super war-clan.

JUNE 2013
Two years after first enlisting to Vortex Security, Lilly_S was deemed worthy of becoming the group leader and was crowned Benevolent Empress.

LATE 2011
Lilly_S went from playing all the awesome games on Roblox to dabbling in scripting for the first time to create her own experiences using the Lua language.

QUICK FACT
Lilly_S is a big fan of showcase designers and loves beautifully crafted worlds like Crykee's Temple of Memories.

LITOZINNAMON

MASTER TACTICIAN OF THE FIRST PERSON SHOOTER GENRE

Wrapped up in his Roblox scarf and armed with his Bluster Buster, litozinnamon is locked, loaded and ready for mortal combat. This accomplished StyLiS Studios game developer has helped to bring to life some of the most-loved and award-winning games on Roblox, including Call of Robloxia 5 and Phantom Forces.

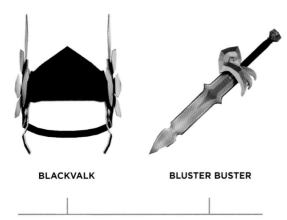

BLACKVALK

BLUSTER BUSTER

CREATOR

DEVELOPER TIMELINE

DECEMBER 2009
After joining the world of Roblox, litozinnamon started to craft his own first-person shooter, Call of Robloxia 5, which was one of the first of its kind on the platform.

JANUARY 2016
Phantom Forces won the prize for Favourite Breakout Game at the Third Annual Bloxy Awards, recognising the achievements of 2015's greatest games.

AUGUST 2014
He stealthily started to create Phantom Forces, which has proven to be one of the most popular games on Roblox, gaining more than a million favourites.

QUICK FACT
He's the owner of the StyLiS Studios game creation group, which has over 185,000 members to date.

LOLERIS

DON'T FALL FOR HIS CHARMING SMILE, THIS DEVELOPER MEANS BUSINESS

This maniacal maker of Mad Games has forged some of the most popular experiences on Roblox, including The Mad Murderer, Darkness and Intense Sword Fighting. loleris is never seen without his Stunna Shades and illuminating smile, because he never knows when he might need to leave a scene of explosive disaster with a smooth, cool swagger.

CREATOR

**BOMBO'S
SURVIVAL KNIFE**

POINTY BOY HAIR

DEVELOPER TIMELINE

FEBRUARY 2009
On his first day on Roblox, this fledgling programmer began to create his very first game, Mad War, which would be the first in his renowned 'Mad' series.

JANUARY 2014
loleris honed his game-dev skills with the 2013 game Darkness, which he then followed up a year later with an even shadier sequel, Darkness 2.

JUNE 2013
loleris's next hit game was the sabre-sharp Intense Sword Fighting, in which over 2 million visitors have sliced-and-diced their way to victory.

NOVEMBER 2014
By the end of 2014, his development group Mad Studios had collaborated to create a series of classic games, including Mad Murderer and Mad Paintball.

LORD UMBERHALLOW

SOME MYSTERIOUS BEINGS JUST WANT TO WATCH THE WORLD BURN

They say on the night of a full Robloxian moon, the ultimate trickster Lord Umberhallow lurks under the cover of darkness and plays his mischievous pranks on unsuspecting passers-by. Whenever you spot a scorching trail of immense fire, you know that this devilish wrongdoer and his faithful fiery blade are never far away.

ROBLOX FAMILY CHARACTER

CRIMSON WINGS

FIERY HORNS OF THE NETHERWORLD

CONJURING MAGIC SPELLS IN ... ELEMENTAL WARS

Being a shadowy trickster, Lord Umberhallow loves messing with the primeval forces of reality. Elemental Wars indulges him by placing the power to command fire, ice, darkness and more in his creepy claws. He has no problem besting the other residents of this magic-imbued world.

GAME STATS

DEVELOPER
Gamer Robot

The studio behind Elemental Wars is Gamer Robot, led by mygame43 and Robotmega. Their first game was Elemental Battlegrounds, a prequel to Elemental Wars, which has gained over 86 million visits.

VISITED

FAVOURITED

MAELSTRONOMER

DEVILISH DEVELOPER WITH AN AWARD-WINNING BACK CATALOGUE

Devoted Robloxian developer Maelstronomer is known for creating hit games such as Super Blocky Ball and Pilgrim Islands Reborn. While his crooked horns look a bit insidious, and his scarlet complexion gives him a devilish style, it's Maelstronomer's wicked grin that ultimately reveals a mischievous nature lurking beneath his striking appearance.

BIGGERHEAD

WARRIOR OF THE THIRD EYE

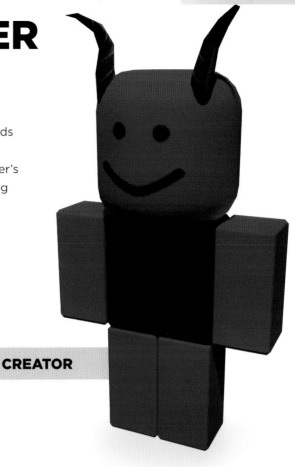

CREATOR

DEVELOPER TIMELINE

SEPTEMBER 2008
Maelstronomer hit the ground running after only a couple of months on Roblox and started work on a couple of games, including Pilgrims Island Reborn.

FEBRUARY 2017
He came away from the 2016 Bloxy Awards with an award for Pilgrim Islands Reborn, which won the award for the game with the Highest Average Playtime.

THE
BLOXYS
2016

JUNE 2014
The devilish dev began to juggle a couple of projects, including racer Super Blocky Ball, which has reached around 20 million eager gamers and counting!

JUNE 2017
PIR became RIP, as Maelstronomer decided to close down the old version of his award-winning game in order to devise a brand new edition.

MATT DUSEK

*PROGRAMMING PHENOMENON WHO MAKES
THE MAGIC HAPPEN BEHIND THE SCENES*

As one of the first to work alongside the pioneering
Builderman, this masterful programmer is a true wizard
of Robloxia. After years of spectral studying, Matt Dusek
has all the magical tools needed to destroy pesky bugs
with the blink of his all-seeing eye. Matt Dusek wears
the all-powerful Dusekkar, which shows off his ultimate
programming power!

ROBLOX CLASSIC

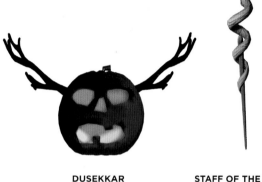

DUSEKKAR   **STAFF OF THE WINDS**

ONE OF HIS FAVOURITE GAMES IS ... SWORD FIGHTS ON THE HEIGHTS IV

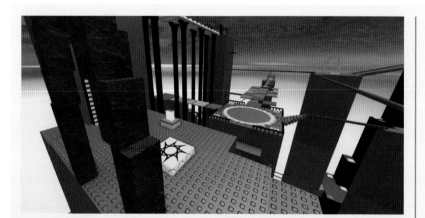

After a busy day scaling the peaks of Robloxia, destroying bugs and
exploiters, Matt Dusek takes time to admire the view and grabs a sword
for a quick session of Shedletsky's Sword Fights on the Heights IV. Players
need nerves of steel to navigate the labyrinth of high-rise stairs, ledges
and platforms ... it's also handy if they possess a sword of steel!

GAME STATS

DEVELOPER
Shedletsky (p. 117)

This popular sword fighting game
has been around for over a decade
and is the brainchild of veteran
Roblox programmer Shedletsky, who
also created the unusually unique
Ride A Cart Into My Face.

VISITED

FAVOURITED

MEEPCITY FISHERMAN

CRAZY-HATTED CITY DWELLER AND ANGLING ENTHUSIAST

At the end of the dock, the MeepCity Fisherman triumphantly casts out his line into the watery depths. He is a figure of patience and calm with a 'reel' talent for catching the big ones! With his trusty Meep by his side and a box full of bait, he never worries if he loses a bite because he knows there are plenty of fish left in the MeepCity pond!

GAME CHARACTER

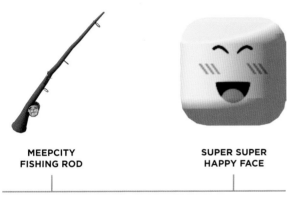

MEEPCITY FISHING ROD

SUPER SUPER HAPPY FACE

GONE FISHIN' IN ... MEEPCITY

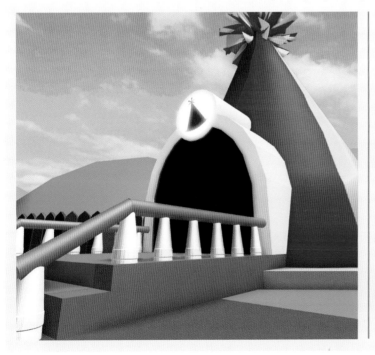

GAME INFORMATION

MeepCity Fisherman is based on the role-play game MeepCity by Alexnewtron, which was the first game to reach a billion visits! In MeepCity there's lots to do – players can throw parties for friends, adopt pet Meeps and furnish their own home. It's also full of fun minigames, like Star Ball and the MeepCity fishing pond, where players can earn money to spend on cool accessories for their adorable Meeps!

DEVELOPER
Alexnewtron (p. 9)

VISITED

FAVOURITED

MERELY

A RENOWNED TREASURE HUNTER WITH HIS EYES ON THE PRIZE

The ultimate connoisseur collector, Merely has scoured the lands of Roblox for its rarest and most prized virtual treasures. Together with his twin brother, Seranok, Merely is world-renowned as being one of the most prolific Roblox developers out there and has created a collector's paradise in Trade Hangout, where virtual items can be traded, swapped and admired.

ROBLOX CLASSIC

MERELY'S SPARKLE TIME HOVERBOARD

DOMINO CROWN

ONE OF HIS FAVOURITE GAMES IS ... WHATEVER FLOATS YOUR BOAT

He may have collected every sought-after item in Robloxia, but does he have his own gun-boat? Well, yes, at least when he's playing one of his favourite games, Whatever Floats Your Boat. Players get to build their own seafaring ship from simple materials, recruit a team of armed comrades to help fend off attackers, and survive the fast-paced combat that ensues in every chaotic round.

GAME STATS

DEVELOPER
Quenty (p. 97)

This mysterious developer has had a prolific dev career on Roblox. Whatever Floats Your Boat is the latest showpiece in a portfolio that also includes Floppy Sword Fish, Sunset Race and Trade Enterprise.

VISITED

FAVOURITED

MICROWAVE SPYBOT

A WALKING, TALKING, GRILLING MACHINE ON A MISSION

The devious Microwave Spybot is the mechanical master of disguise. Just when you thought it was safe to go back into the kitchen, this espionage android will distract you with his convenient microwave unit. He'll extract your top-secret recipes while you heat up those mouth-watering leftovers, and upload them to his culinary mainframe.

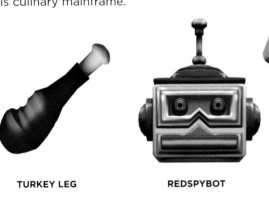

TURKEY LEG   **REDSPYBOT**

TRAINING TO BE A MASTER CHEF IN ... RESTAURANT TYCOON

Microwave Spybot makes full use of his appliance disguise in his favourite building game on Roblox, Restaurant Tycoon. With all his undercover-cooking experience, Spybot loves running his own restaurant, taking orders, cooking up treats and collecting tips. He also loves to wander around other shops for some interior design inspiration!

GAME STATS

DEVELOPER
Ultraw

This full-flavoured simulation has attracted nearly 120 million visits from hungry gamers and is one of developer Ultraw's many successful tycoon offerings, including Pizza Factory and Gym Island.

VISITED

FAVOURITED

MR. BLING BLING

GENTLEMAN CLAD IN GOLD ATTIRE, WITH A DAZZLING PERSONALITY TO MATCH

When it comes to pure glitz and glamour, Mr. Bling Bling is your man. With a flashy smile and a tailored suit woven from the finest gold linens his extreme wealth can buy, he enjoys showing off his extravagant fashion sense to any Robloxian who will stop and stare. His excessive lifestyle may not be very subtle, but when did subtlety ever buy anyone fortune and fame?

ROBLOX FAMILY CHARACTER

GOLDEN STAFF OF BLING SQUARED

GOLDEN TOP HAT OF BLING BLING

DIGGING FOR GOLD IN ... EPIC MINING 2

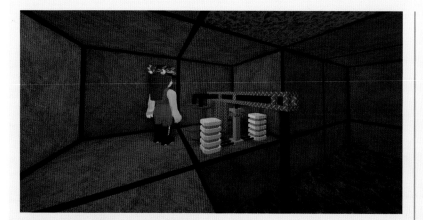

Mr. Bling Bling can't stop himself from hoarding riches, even when he's trying to relax, so he skips the merchants and middlemen and heads straight to the source in Epic Mining 2. He chops down trees and sells the timber and decimates mines with dynamite to collect precious ores that he can sell for a pretty profit.

GAME STATS

DEVELOPER
QuintinityZero

Released in the early days of 2010, Epic Mining 2 was the first step in QuintinityZero's game development career. Over 14 million miners have taken up their pickaxe and visited his simulation game since release.

VISITED

FAVOURITED

MR. ROBOT

ONLY ONE CONDUCTOR SHORT OF A COMPLETE CIRCUIT

Is he a real robot or just a man with a cardboard box on his head? Maybe he's a Noob in an unconvincing disguise? This mysterious Robloxian is truly an enigma, and we may never decode Mr. Robot's true identity. What we do know is he's no hero or saviour, he's just a normal man-dressed-as-a-robot/robot-pretending-to-be-a-man, whose circuits are out of control!

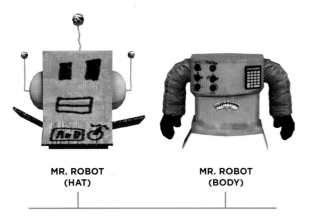

MR. ROBOT (HAT)

MR. ROBOT (BODY)

ROBLOX FAMILY CHARACTER

INITIATING A NUCLEAR MELTDOWN IN ... INNOVATION LABS

To escape the funny looks he gets walking around in the real world, Mr. Robot likes the anonymity he can enjoy in the nuclear meltdown thriller Innovation Labs. Here he goes by the name of Professor Robot, and you can find him carrying out one of various experiments – teleporting food, mutating employees and whizzing around on his brand new jetpack ... the best Robux he's ever spent!

GAME STATS

DEVELOPER

madattak

The interactive complex of Innovation Labs is straight out of developer madattak's imagination. He's welcomed over 18 million visitors to his not-so-secret underground lab.

VISITED

FAVOURITED

MYZTA

ARTIST EXTRAORDINAIRE EMBARKING ON AN UNDERWATER ADVENTURE

A kind-hearted developer, Myzta's love for sculpting imaginative pieces of 3D art is readily apparent in all her amazing Roblox creations. The tireless Myzta is always busy working on a multitude of new and fantastic games and experiences, including From the Deep, which will transport players on an epic quest through the dark and mysterious depths of the sea.

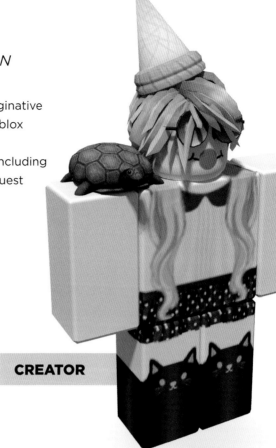

STRAWBERRY ICE CREAM HAIR

TURTLE SHOULDER FRIEND

CREATOR

DEVELOPER TIMELINE

EARLY 2012
Myzta's love of playing games slowly morphed into modelling assets and tweaking existing games to make them more fun for her friends to play.

QUICK FACT
In the early years, Myzta loved playing building games against her friends ... which explains why she's now such an awesome modeller!

EARLY 2014
After playing lots of cool Roblox games, Myzta decided to start developing her own games and she set forth on her path of modelling genius!

QUICK FACT
She's currently hard at work on a new game called BitterSweet. It's a frantic multiplayer battle game based in a land made of candy! Sweet!

NEIGHBORHOOD OF ROBLOXIA: MAYOR

A POLITICAL POWERHOUSE OF ROBLOXIAN GOVERNMENT

After a political career littered with smear campaigns, corruption and blocky dealings, Neighborhood of Robloxia Mayor finally seized power as the Robloxian of the people. She's the mayor of one of the most popular role-play experiences on Roblox, and she's on an ideological crusade to make sure the neighborhood is the perfect place to play!

GAME CHARACTER

PRESIDENTIAL VAMPIRE SLAYING AX

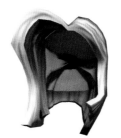

SHOULDER LENGTH BLONDE HAIR

REGULATING AND LEGISLATING IN ... NEIGHBORHOOD OF ROBLOXIA

GAME INFORMATION

The Mayor governs the not-so-mean streets of The Neighborhood of Robloxia. Designed by Q_Q, this open-world game lets players choose from dozens of jobs, earn money and find a home, which can be customised with various furnishings. They can also roam the huge map, buy cars and interact with their fellow Robloxians. The game has hit over 100 million visits since 2012, making it developer Q_Q's most popular creation to date.

DEVELOPER
Q_Q

VISITED

FAVOURITED

NEIGHBORHOOD OF ROBLOXIA SHERIFF

KICKING BLOX AND TAKING NAMES IS ALL IN A DAY'S WORK

Watch out, there's a new sheriff in town and he's had it up to his Robloxian hat of justice with the bad guys dragging his neighborhood down. Armed with his trusted sidearm and handcuffs of righteousness, he's always on patrol in his super-fast cruiser, and will stop at nothing to bring law and order to The Neighborhood of Robloxia.

GAME CHARACTER

POLICE BADGE

NEW SHERIFF IN TOWN

KEEPING THE PEACE IN ... NEIGHBORHOOD OF ROBLOXIA

GAME INFORMATION

Sheriff is one of the roles that players can take on in The Neighborhood of Robloxia. You can choose to work for the police as a normal cop or as part of a SWAT unit. Players can drive a patrol car and wield a gun as well as a pair of handcuffs, which allows them to hunt down criminals. There are lots of other jobs in the game, too, including teacher, firefighter, doctor and student ... or if you want you can be unemployed!

DEVELOPER
Q_Q

VISITED

FAVOURITED

NEVERLAND LAGOON: TEIYIA

QUEEN OF THE LAGOON AND RULER OF A MAGICAL EMPIRE

This inhabitant of the magical Neverland Lagoon can more often than not be found sitting atop the waterfall of the eponymous body of water, surveying her kingdom. She may be a mermaid, but in the Neverland Lagoon, she, along with King SelDraken, has dominion over the entire realm.

GAME CHARACTER

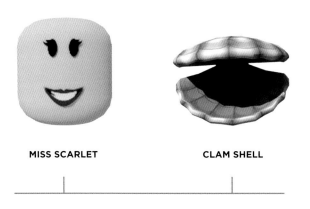

MISS SCARLET

CLAM SHELL

BENEVOLENT RULER OF ... NEVERLAND LAGOON

GAME INFORMATION

Neverland Lagoon: Teiyia reigns supreme over SelDraken and Teiyia's Neverland Lagoon. The game has dozens of areas to explore and hidden treasures to discover. Visitors to the magical game can create a new character and add morphs like mermaid tails, fairy wings and much more, allowing them to role-play as different fantastical beings. You can even adopt a pet from the stables outside the castle.

DEVELOPER
SelDraken (p. 113) & Teiyia (p. 127)

VISITED

FAVOURITED

NEXX

UBIQUITOUS DIGIPUNK DEV OF THE ROBLOX COMMUNITY

This steampunk developer thrives across the digital landscape, from community-supporting websites to gaming wonderlands. Nexx's coding skills earned him the RDC 2016 Game Jam award, and he's currently working on an epic follow-up to Roblox Reviews, a popular website that combines the aggregate review scores of classic Roblox games from the community and critics alike.

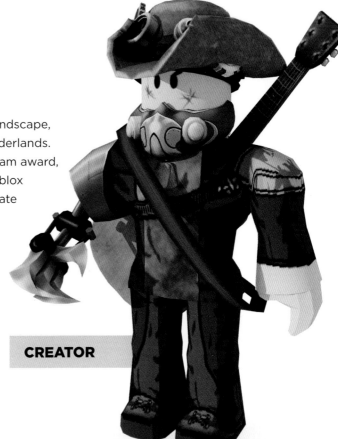

CREATOR

NOMADIC STEAMPUNK HEADBAND

GUITAR BACKPACK

DEVELOPER TIMELINE

AUGUST 2016
Nexx created the development group Mammoth Creative, and in the same month released the first game under the banner, Zookeeper Tycoon.

QUICK FACT
When Nexx first dabbled on Roblox, the type of games he most liked to play were obbys, like The Really Easy Obby.

DECEMBER 2017
Nexx has been furiously developing the new card battling game Clashblox Heroes, which was previously released on Roblox as a playable alpha.

QUICK FACT
He was part of the legendary Roblox intern program and spent time in the secret kingdom that is ... Roblox HQ!

NICK

PART HUMAN, PART HORSE, BUT COMPLETELY CRAZY

He's a man with a horse's head, on a mad mission to accomplish his lifelong aspiration of world domination. Nick knows he's got one chance at life ... you only live once, and he needs to execute his master plan and survive the ultimate Roblox experience of Mad Games ... that is, until he respawns and tries again!

GAME CHARACTER

MAD MURDERER KNIFE

I'LL HAVE ANOTHER

ONLY LIVES ONCE IN ... ULTIMATE DRIVING: WESTOVER ISLANDS

Delaying world domination for some downtime, Nick likes to let off steam behind the wheel in the ultimate driving experience on Roblox, Ultimate Driving: Westover Islands. He's racked up nearly 25,000 fast-and-furious miles and has treated himself to a really red Diablo.

GAME STATS

DEVELOPER
TwentyTwoPilots

This popular driving sim is part of the Ultimate Driving series, created by TwentyTwoPilots, the Developer and Builder of the Year in 2016. Each game is focused on a new area to cruise around and explore.

VISITED

FAVOURITED

NOOB007

HE'S GOT A LICENSE TO THRILL AND THE SQL SKILLS TO PAY THE BILLS

On first glance, you might mistake this Robloxian as an easy-prey debutant, but he is in fact a hardened veteran with a licence to thrill. Noob007 is also dressed to kill with his own specially tailored hat, the Crown of the Dark Lord of SQL, which endows him with the power of an ancient data language that was once thought lost to the mists of time.

ROBLOX CLASSIC

CROWN OF THE DARK LORD OF SQL

NOOBTUBE

ONE OF HIS FAVOURITE GAMES IS ... NATURAL DISASTER SURVIVAL

Noob007 is used to striking fear into his foes, but he isn't the only thing inspiring terror in the hearts of Robloxians when he jumps into his favourite Roblox game, Natural Disaster Survival. He's become a pro over his years of playing, and is able to expertly evade everything from gigantic tsunamis to spewing volcanoes. Every now and again, he likes to take the challenge up a notch and set up a multi-disaster game, which really separates the noobs from the pros.

GAME STATS

DEVELOPER
Stickmasterluke (p. 121)

Natural Disaster Survival was the first game that Stickmasterluke released on Roblox over a decade ago in 2008. It's maintained its popularity over the years and gained over half a billion visits!

VISITED

FAVOURITED

NOOBERTUBER

*THE BATTLE-HARDENED BANE
OF THE ROBLOXIAN NEWCOMER*

Decked out in his foreboding black full-body armour,
Noobertuber is always ready for battle. He is known
throughout the kingdom of Robloxia for his legendary combat
skills, which have made him a fighting force to be reckoned
with. His rare helmet was awarded to him in recognition of his
elite fighting prowess at the 2007 Grand Melee competition.

**CLASSIC SWORDPACK
THROWBACK**

**THE KLEOS
APHTHITON**

CREATOR

DEVELOPER TIMELINE

AUGUST 2007
Noobertuber received
one of four glorious Kleos
Aphthiton helmets after
triumphing at the Grand
Melee, knocking out 137
competitors along the way.

JANUARY 2018
Noobertuber gained a new
frame of reference when he
began to shape his gravity-
altering game Reference
Shift. It's a work in progress
that's certainly worth a look.

JANUARY 2008
After spending a year
exploring the wonders
that Roblox had to offer,
Noobertuber started work
on his classic optical-
challenge game Refraction.

QUICK FACT
He belongs to the
Roblox Wiki group
and contributes to the
smooth running of the
extremely useful online
community resource.

OFFICER ZOMBIE

LAW ENFORCER IN HOT PURSUIT OF JUSTICE AND HUMAN FLESH

Braaains ... doughnuuuts! This enforcer of the undead law has quite an appetite for justice! Whether he's out and about stumbling after criminals or commanding a horde of bloodthirsty undead, Officer Zombie always has time to drop in for a snack with the law-abiding locals. Just be careful he doesn't put you on the menu!

ROBLOX FAMILY CHARACTER

OFFICER ZOMBIE

POLICE BATON

GOING ON THE OFFENSIVE IN ... KICK OFF

After a night of mindlessly staggering through the mean streets, Officer Zombie makes the most of his leisure time by supporting his favourite game, Kick Off! Officer Zombie can leave his brain in the locker room and run around like a headless Robloxian chasing a ball around a field ... Watch out for his biting tackle!

GAME STATS

DEVELOPER
CM Games

With over 59 million visits and more than 400,000 favourites, this sports classic by CM Games and lead developer Lethal682 is perfect for getting a quick game in with your football friends!

VISITED

FAVOURITED

THE OVERSEER

AN EVIL OVERLORD WITH MORE THAN A DOZEN EYES ON THE PRIZE

What does the future hold? Who will lay claim to the ultimate victory in the battle of the ages? What are next week's winning lottery numbers? Only The Overseer knows the answers! With his all-seeing eye, this prophet of pure evil helps mastermind the Korbloxian army, and what he lacks in depth perception, he more than makes up in fortune-telling!

ROBLOX FAMILY CHARACTER

OVERSEER'S BOW

OVERSEER'S AXE

MOSTLY SEEKING IN ... HIDE AND SEEK EXTREME

Having so many eyes at his disposal gives The Overseer a great advantage in some games, like his favourite Hide and Seek Extreme. One player is chosen to be 'It' and is tasked with finding the other players who are hiding in huge maps. Nothing gets past The Overseer's many eyes though, and he finds everyone, every time. He's pretty good at hiding, too!

GAME STATS

DEVELOPER
Tim7775 (p. 129)

The master developer behind this super-fun seek-'em-up is Tim7775. This heroic creator is also responsible for the competitive construction game Building Frenzy, which was recently remastered.

VISITED

FAVOURITED

PHANTOM FORCES: GHOST

HIGHLY-TRAINED COMMANDO ARMED TO THE HILT AND READY FOR ACTION

The commander of Task Force Blox is the ultimate Special Forces operative and has led hundreds of highly classified missions in the classic Roblox game Phantom Forces. He's trained in an arsenal of specialised weapons and wrote the rulebook on combat tactics. If you have a problem, if no one else can help and if you can find him ... maybe you can hire this highly-trained operative.

GAME CHARACTER

1ST BATTALION RED DEVIL'S BERET

RED SERIOUS SCAR FACE

STORMING COMPOUNDS IN ... PHANTOM FORCES

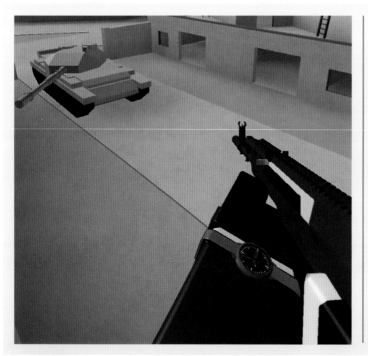

GAME INFORMATION

This member of the Ghost faction is an elite marksman in the co-op shooter Phantom Forces, by StyLiS Studios, which boasts more than 365 million visits. In Phantom Forces, players join one of two teams, the Phantoms and the Ghosts, and go head-to-head in a range of frantic, all-action game modes. The game has a range of weapons to arm your soldier with and features unique movement controls including sliding and diving.

DEVELOPER
StyLiS Studios

VISITED

FAVOURITED

PIXEL ARTIST

CREATIVE CHARACTER ADEPT AT MAKING MASTERPIECES AS WELL AS MESSES

This prodigy of artistic proportions has an intense desire to draw in the classic drawing game Pixel Art Creator, which has amassed a gallery of pixelated masterpieces. With a palette of rainbow hair and a paint-splattered dress-sense, Pixel Artist is on the cutting-edge of the Robloxian art scene and is always pushing the boundaries of geometric arty-ness.

GAME CHARACTER

WILD AND CRAZY HAIR

HEEEEEEY...

BASICALLY LIVES IN ... PIXEL ART CREATOR

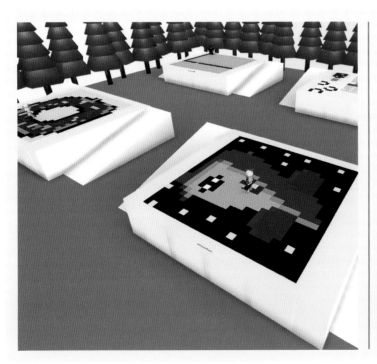

GAME INFORMATION

The Pixel Artist character is based on the blocky drawing experience Pixel Art Creator. The retro-art game has notched up over 10 million visits since 2012. Pixel Art Creator allows the artist inside us all to come out in the form of simple pixel drawings. Players are given large blank canvases to block-out with a palette of colours, creating their very own pixelated masterpiece to show off to their Robloxian friends.

DEVELOPER
Pixel Art Creator Community

VISITED

FAVOURITED

PIXELATEDCANDY

STYLISH DEVELOPER WITH A PASSION FOR FASHION

Do you need a little help with your runway walk, or some advice on your wardrobe? PixelatedCandy is the fashionista developer behind one of the most popular fashion games on Roblox – Fashion Famous! She has an aesthetic eye for all things fashion and knows every top tip and creative cheat that will turn you into a style goddess!

PINK SPARKLE TIME FEDORA

ELVEN DRUID

CREATOR

DEVELOPER TIMELINE

JUNE 2014
PixelatedCandy first discovered the sweet brilliance of the Roblox platform and joined up to enjoy some blox-filled fun and games.

ROBLOX

JUN 2014

DECEMBER 2016
She gave her fans the ability to take fashion on the move by creating a mobile version of Fashion Frenzy, which has now been visited more times than the original!

NOVEMBER 2016
This sugar-coated developer started working on her standout style classic, Fashion Frenzy, which lets users dress to impress other players and win a prize.

QUICK FACT
In 2017 PixelatedCandy revisited Fashion Frenzy with a new-and-improved update and changed the name of the game to Fashion Famous.

PIZZA DELIVERY GUY

SERVICE WITH A SMILE, THIS GUY ALWAYS DELIVERS THE GOODS

When business hours are coming to an end and you have dozens of hot, delicious pizzas to deliver to hungry, impatient customers, there's only one pro you need to call ... Pizza Delivery Guy! There's nothing he likes more than to skillfully balance a stack of perfectly made pizzas on the back of his scooter while he cruises around town looking cool.

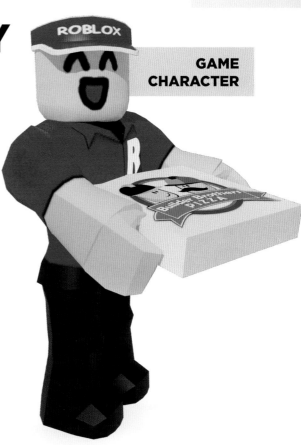

GAME CHARACTER

PIZZA DELIVERY VEHICLE

2007 ROBLOX VISOR

SLINGING PIZZA PIES IN ... WORK AT A PIZZA PLACE

GAME INFORMATION

Pizza Delivery Guy is a character based on the hugely popular Work at a Pizza Place, developed by Dued1. You can choose to take on one of five roles at Builder Brothers Pizza's flagship store, from serving hungry customers and cooking up delicious pizzas, to delivering hot treats to homes, just like Pizza Delivery Guy. Whichever role you opt for in Work at a Pizza Place, you'll always get to wear the snazzy red uniform.

DEVELOPER
Dued1 (p. 38)

VISITED

FAVOURITED

93

PLAYROBOT

GAMER-TURNED-DEVELOPER WITH A PENCHANT FOR ALL THINGS ANIMAL

This playful developer is one of the early pioneers in role-playing experiences on Roblox. Playrobot's popular 2008 hit Robloxaville was the first hit-stop on her gaming journey, and she soon followed it up with Lakeside in 2012, the first game to reach one million visits. Together, her iconic games have racked up a staggering 10 million visits and counting!

TYRANNOSAURUS

AQUA DRAGON TAIL

DEVELOPER TIMELINE

DECEMBER 2007
Playrobot discovered the undeniable awesomeness of Roblox a mere year after it was first released and signed up as quickly as she possibly could.

ROBLOX

DEC 2007

JANUARY 2012
After four years of playing games and keeping on top of development on Robloxaville, Playrobot released her next role-playing classic, Lakeside.

MARCH 2008
Early on in her Roblox experience, Playrobot created the seminal role-play game Robloxaville, which has attracted more than 8 million visits.

QUICK FACT
Playrobot is a famous dev on the platform and has more than 65,000 followers on Roblox.

PYROLYSIS

FIERY ROBLOX INTERN, KNOWN FOR TIP-TOP TOP HATS AND MANY PAST USERNAMES

If you look at this Roblox creator's name badge and think his moniker is just for show then you thought wrong! Pyrolysis possesses a supernatural volcanic ability that allows him to shoot fire and set anything ablaze. But don't worry, he only uses his hot touch for the powers of good ... most of the time!

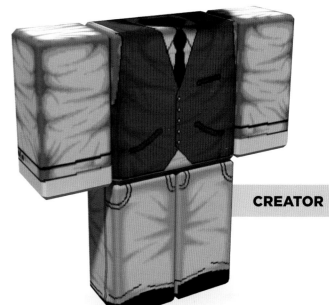

CREATOR

ADURITE CLOCKWORK SHADES

RED BANDED TOP HAT

DEVELOPER TIMELINE

EARLY 2011

After a couple of years immersing himself in the wonders of Roblox, Pyrolysis joined the famous Vortex Security clan, with aspirations of greatness.

JULY 2015

He started to work on his jetpack-fuelled, neon-lit fighting game, Tiny Titans, under the banner of his newly-created development group Pyro's Cult.

MAY 2013

As the young Pyrolysis became a teenager in the real world, he picked up some Lua skills and transformed into a fiery developer on Roblox!

LATE 2017

He joined the illustrious list of successful developers who have taken part in the Roblox intern program and got to peek inside the blox-ilicious gates of Roblox HQ!

QUEEN OF THE TREELANDS

BENEVOLENT MONARCH WHO RULES THE VERDANT FOREST DOMAIN

As the seasons turn across the picturesque TreeLands, the mighty Queen presides over her realm and sends blessings to all who come and play in NewFissy's treetop tycoon. With her glorious Autumn Staff that has been passed down through the royal generations, the Queen of the TreeLands wields her divine power with fairness and grace.

WINGS OF AUTUMN   AUTUMN OAK STAFF

GAME CHARACTER

REIGNING OVER ... TREELANDS

GAME INFORMATION

Queen of the TreeLands reigns supreme over NewFissy's TreeLands, which has over 9 million visits. In TreeLands, gamers get to build a tree house, adding sections as they earn resources and money. To increase their wealth, residents roam the realm and pick fruit from the forest of plenty. They can then use their wealth to procure harvesting machines, useful vehicles and build the tree house of their dreams!

DEVELOPER
NewFissy

VISITED

FAVOURITED

QUENTY

OMNIPRESENT BUILDER KNOWN FOR HELPING OTHERS REALISE THEIR DREAMS

This expert developer may look like a mischievous bandit, but he has a Robin Hood nature to his programming ways, offering a helping hand to other developers as they create awesome play experiences. Quenty has a reputation for being one of the greatest Robloxian builders and when he's not helping others, he's working on one of his most popular games, Whatever Floats Your Boat.

DELUXE BANDIT MASK

FRUMPLED WIZARD HAT OF OLD COOTS

CREATOR

DEVELOPER TIMELINE

JUNE 2011
He began work forging the place that would eventually become Trade Enterprise, a seafaring adventure that has players assume the role of daring travelling merchants.

MAY 2014
Quenty floated his idea for a new game about boatbuilding and heads seaward once more to create survival classic Whatever Floats Your Boat.

OCTOBER 2011
Quenty proved his worth as a paintballing superstar during the Roblox Halloween event, sniping his way to victory and receiving a fancy MVP trophy.

JULY 2017
Quenty attended the Roblox Developers Conference and won an RDC Game Jam trophy for third place with fellow developers Defaultio, Biostream, Crykee and badcc.

RED

MYSTERIOUS MOTORIST OF THE POST-APOCALYPTIC LANDSCAPE

This survival specialist knows a thing or two about living with the undead. Red doesn't need a handbook to know that to outwit the zombie hordes, she needs just two things – speed and firepower! Luckily, these are the two things Red has in abundance, with her handy rifle and all-terrain 4x4. At the end of the apocalyptic day, if you can't shoot them, run them down!

GAME CHARACTER

RED BEANIE AND BLONDE HAIR

M1 GARAND

HOARDING JERRY CANS IN ... APOCALYPSE RISING 2

GAME INFORMATION

Hailing from the post-apocalyptic wasteland of Apocalypse Rising, Red is a survivor with a dream of a better world, which has steered her towards the sequel, Apocalypse Rising 2. With her penchant for zombie lore and encyclopedic survival knowledge, she was the perfect person to put the improved GUI through its paces, explore new maps and dabble in a little troubleshooting, while killing a few zombies along the way.

DEVELOPER
Dualpoint Interactive

VISITED

FAVOURITED

RED LAZER PARKOUR RUNNER

BOUNDLESS ENERGY AND A STOCKED LOADOUT MAKE HIM A FORMIDABLE FOE

With a smooth tuxedo-style and a flash of red hair, Red LAZER Parkour Runner is more than ready for the slash-and-shoot, high-octane action in the classic fighting game, LAZER. His parkour skills allow him to evade and creep up on his prey, while his vast knowledge of weaponry makes him a killer foe who is also partial to an awesome power-up!

RED AWESOME HAIR

RED ROCK STAR SMILE

ONLY PLAYS AS OVERDRIVE IN ... HEROES OF ROBLOXIA

GAME INFORMATION

Red LAZER Parkour Runner can usually be found in MasterOfTheElements's all-action, combat game LAZER, but when he's not free-running, he relaxes between rounds and plays another classic Roblox game, Heroes of Robloxia. In this comic book-inspired RPG, players choose a hero, each with a different superpower, then team up and head into Roblox City to battle the forces of evil and try to defeat the supervillain Darkmatter!

DEVELOPER
Team Super

VISITED

FAVOURITED

REDCLIFF ELITE COMMANDER

THE SHARP POINT AT THE TIP OF REDCLIFF'S MILITARY EMPIRE

When evil casts a shadow of war and misery on the kingdom of Robloxia, the Redcliff Elite Commander stands as a beacon of justice and light. He heroically leads his legions of elite knights on their grand quest to rid the kingdom of all evil and strives to bring peace and liberty to the land.

**KNIGHTS OF REDCLIFF:
SWORD AND SHIELD**

**REDCLIFF ELITE
COMMANDER HELMET**

FIGHTING FIRE WITH FIRE IN ... DRAGONVS

Heroic knights like Redcliff Elite Commander are famous for their dragon-slaying abilities. However, he likes to rebel against this stereotype by playing DragonVS, a scaly simulator game that puts him in control of a fearsome fire-breather. He spends his time roasting defenseless sheep, collecting masses of coins and soaring through the skies of a strange land. Luckily, he hasn't encountered any knights on his travels ... yet.

GAME STATS

DEVELOPER
ChickenEngineer

This clucky developer released DragonVS into the Roblox wilds in 2017. Over half a million players assumed control of an awesome wyvern in the first six months of release, and more will surely follow.

VISITED

FAVOURITED

REESEMCBLOX

*THE UNICORN-HORNED CORNERSTONE
OF THE ROBLOX COMMUNITY TEAM*

There are few Robloxians that are more dedicated to the Roblox community than ReeseMcBlox. As one of the earliest employees at Roblox, she has devoted her Robloxian life to improving the platform every day. Some say her magical unicorn horn allows her to summon a pony whenever she needs one ... so you might see her galloping home after a busy day at the office.

ROBLOX CLASSIC

HIPSTER GLASSES　　　　**UNICORN HORN**

ONE OF HER FAVOURITE GAMES IS ... VOLT

After a busy day tending to the Roblox community, ReeseMcBlox dons a radiant jumpsuit ready for a session on one of her favourite games, Volt. The sci-fi battle-bike classic tests ReeseMcBlox's guile, reactions and wit in a duel of fast cars, neon walls and insane jumps. She also loves playing the retro 2D arcade machines in the game's lobby while she awaits her next challenger!

GAME STATS

DEVELOPER

TeamVolt

This TeamVolt gem, another collaboration between asimo3089 and badcc, takes its gameplay and visual influences from retro gaming and sci-fi classics, and has attracted over 7 million visits to date.

VISITED

FAVOURITED

RIPULL

CREATIVE DEVELOPER WITH AS MANY TALENTS AS HE HAS MINIGAMES

Avoiding explosive mines ... dodging grotesque zombies and combatting burly gladiators ... you name it and you'll find it in one of Ripull's awesome games! This creative mastermind loves a zany, action-packed Roblox adventure and has been creating such experiences for more than nine years, racking up over 100 million visits to his high-octane experiences!

CREATOR

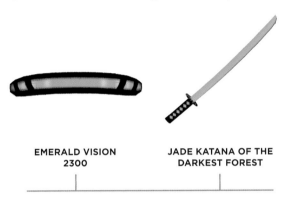

EMERALD VISION
2300

JADE KATANA OF THE
DARKEST FOREST

DEVELOPER TIMELINE

SUMMER 2010
Ripull started his game development engine and sped off to make Roblox Derby, which later spawned the 2012 sequel Roblox Derby 2.

JULY 2015
Ripull started work on the spiritual successor to his compilation hit and released Ripull's Games, which has attracted over 10 million visits to date.

SEPTEMBER 2014
A professed gaming fanatic, Ripull used his gaming know-how and started to create his most popular game to date, the addictive Ripull's Minigames.

QUICK FACT
The Ripull Minigames group, created by the developer himself, has over 50,000 fanatical members.

ROBLOX MODEL

THE SWAGGERING, STYLISH KING OF THE CATWALK

With the perfect runway walk, this Roblox top model has the sass and style to wear anything, from the frilly and fabulous to the cute and charming. Roblox Model is the muse for many famous Robloxian fashion designers who have dared challenge their creativity in the ultimate arena of style, Top Roblox Runway Model.

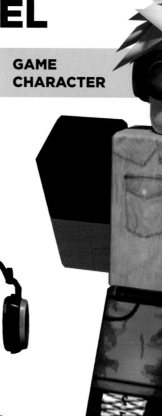

GAME CHARACTER

MIDNIGHT SHADES   **DJ HEADPHONES**

OWNING THE RUNWAY IN ... TOP ROBLOX RUNWAY MODEL

GAME INFORMATION

This style guru is at home strutting down the catwalk of fashion challenge Top Roblox Runway Model. The game has attracted a massive following with over 570,000 favourites. In the game, fashionistas compete against each other in themed rounds. With 100 seconds to dash around the wardrobe room, models must choose an outfit that epitomises the theme before taking to the runway.

DEVELOPER
DizzyPurple (p. 35)

VISITED

FAVOURITED

ROBLOX SKATING RINK

PSYCHEDELIC SOCIAL BUTTERFLY IS THE QUEEN OF THE RINK

This smooth-skating style icon of the rollerblading scene is the glam rock star of the popular hangout game, Roblox Skating Rink. Her punk rock hairstyle and aerodynamic neon spandex give her a killer style that she loves to show off on social media in the thousands of selfies she snaps as she skates!

GAME CHARACTER

RAINBOW CLUB KID HAIR

RAINBOW CAT TAIL

SNAPPING ROLLER-SELFIES IN ... ROBLOX SKATING RINK

GAME INFORMATION

This glittering glider is from johnnygadget's Roblox Skating Rink, which has achieved over 225,000 favourites to date. Visitors can hang out at the arcade and chat with friends at the cafe, as well as grab a pair of skates and cruise the roller disco, pulling off some awesome dance moves as they glide and move in time to the pumping soundtrack. They can also snap the perfect selfie to remember their rocking rink experience!

DEVELOPER

johnnygadget

VISITED

FAVOURITED

ROBLOX STAFF

UNSUNG HERO BEHIND THE SCENES, MAKING ROBLOX A GREAT EXPERIENCE

Fear not, humble Robloxian, Team Roblox is here to save the day! This noble staffer is ready to join in on every amazing gaming adventure, prepared to collect all things limited and awesome, and can't wait to get started on Roblox's next BIG thing ... whatever it may be. Roblox Staff is your go-to guide for everything Roblox!

ROBLOX FAMILY CHARACTER

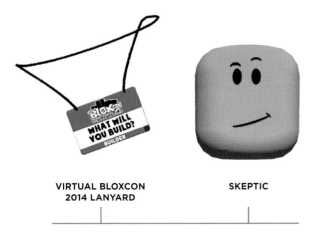

VIRTUAL BLOXCON 2014 LANYARD

SKEPTIC

ALWAYS UP FOR A FRIENDLY MATCH IN ... ROBLOX FLIP CARDS

Roblox Staff is the complete team player, but has a competitive streak just like everyone else. After a hard day at work, the go-to game for letting off some steam is the frantic card-battle game Roblox Flip Cards. Roblox Staff might be an approachable person most of the time, but when someone dares to approach the Flip Card table, you can be certain that they'll be walking away defeated and empty-handed.

GAME STATS

DEVELOPER

Gamer Robot

Gamer Robot, helmed by mygame43, is the studio behind Roblox Flip Cards. The dev group is also known for the magic role-play Elemental Battlegrounds, which has received over 86 million visits.

VISITED

FAVOURITED

ROBLOX SUPER FAN

YOU THOUGHT YOU LOVED ROBLOX?
NOT AS MUCH AS THIS YOUNG MAN!

By day and by night, and then by day again, this young and enthusiastic fan can always be found on Roblox, playing and chatting with his friends on their latest Robloxian adventure. Roblox Super Fan is a dreamer at heart and is known for being uber enthusiastic about all things bloxy and brilliant!

ROBLOX FAMILY CHARACTER

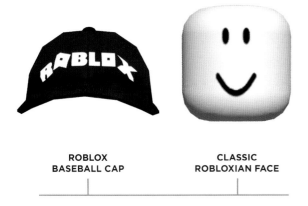

ROBLOX BASEBALL CAP

CLASSIC ROBLOXIAN FACE

LOCKING UP CRIMINALS IN ... JAILBREAK

Roblox Super Fan is super-fanatical about one of the most successful and popular games on Roblox, Jailbreak. In this award-winning crime adventure, Roblox Super Fan prefers to assume the role of a police officer, chasing the crafty cons who are trying to break out and restart their lives of crime on the outside, and capturing those who have already escaped into the lawless world beyond.

GAME STATS

DEVELOPER
Badimo (p. 11)

This hit by game creation group Badimo, comprised of asimo3089 and badcc, is one of the most visited games on Roblox and was the first game to reach the 3 million favourites milestone.

VISITED

FAVOURITED

ROBLOX UNIVERSITY PROFESSOR

SHE'S A ROBLOX GENIUS WHOSE CLASSES ARE ALWAYS A BLAST

Now, you at the back, are you listening carefully? This wise and wacky Roblox University Professor has a reputation for madcap lessons and mesmerising seminars. When she's not setting her hair on fire or blowing up Bunsen burners, she's lecturing on her all-time, number-one subject matter: the theory of blowing everything up!

ROBLOX FAMILY CHARACTER

COOL SCIENTIST

SUPER SPEEDY PURPLE POTION

UNCOVERING ANCIENT MYSTERIES IN ... DINOSAUR SIMULATOR

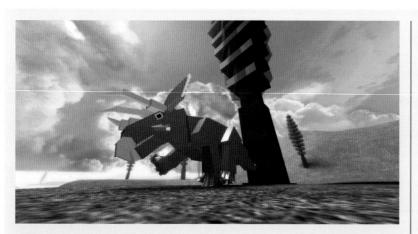

Roblox University Professor knows everything there is to know about paleontology, and she puts all her wisdom to good use in her number-one game on Roblox, Dinosaur Simulator. With a variety of dinosaurs to assume control of, including those that go by air and by sea, there's plenty to keep even the most academic of visitors busy.

GAME STATS

DEVELOPER
ChickenEngineer

This developer is anything but bird-brained. Dinosaur Simulator is still a work in progress, but ChickenEngineer has also released DragonVS, which once again pits scaly beasts against each other.

VISITED

FAVOURITED

ROBLOX UNIVERSITY STUDENT

DEDICATED, HARDWORKING AND EAGER TO LEARN THE ROBLOXIAN WAY

He's only been at Roblox University for a week and Roblox University Student is proving to be the model scholar. When this studious freshman isn't cramming in a huge study-fest in the library, he's on campus happily cheering on the other young students as they build, craft and develop the games of the future.

ROBLOX FAMILY CHARACTER

SHAGGY

BRACES

RACING TO THE FINISH LINE IN ... SUPER BLOCKY BALL

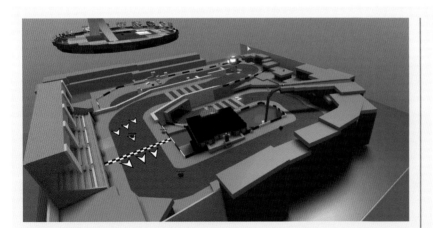

This student of all things Roblox likes a challenge, and he discovered a mega-fun one during his first days at Roblox University! Super Blocky Ball puts your avatar in a ball, which you must navigate through worlds full of obstacles. Mastery of the ball demands balance and hours of free time, but luckily Roblox University Student has these in abundance!

GAME STATS

DEVELOPER
Maelstronomer (p. 71)

This devilish developer is responsible for some of the most fun experiences on Roblox, including the platformer-battle hybrid Wobbly Brickbattle and the spooky maze Hollow Mansion.

VISITED

FAVOURITED

ROCKSTAR

*AN INNATE ABILITY TO SHRED GUITAR
ROCKETED HIM TO ROCK-GOD STATUS*

Born with a guitar in one hand and an amp in the other, Rockstar was raised on rock and roll. A shredder of the nth degree with an axe that has slain even the most mighty of rock gods, Rockstar is a riff idol who can't resist an ultimate jam session. Just his presence inspires all to air-guitar and headbang!

FAMOUS BLOXSTAR
HAIR

FAMOUS BLOXSTAR
GUITAR

ROBLOX FAMILY
CHARACTER

PLAYING TO A SOLD-OUT CROWD IN ... CLONE TYCOON 2

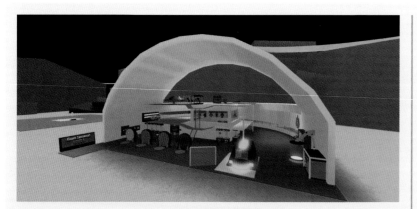

It's hard being a rock god, and it's even harder to find bandmates of equal talent and awesomeness. The solution is theoretically simple, but technically difficult – cloning! Rockstar started to clone himself in the intergalactic Clone Tycoon 2 in 2016, and hasn't held an audition since. He's even given up making music for the time being, concentrating his energy on building the biggest and best army in the galaxy instead!

GAME STATS

DEVELOPER
Ultraw

This battle sim has attracted over 100 million visits and been favourited more than 1 million times, although it's unknown how many of those visits are by clones of developer Ultraw!

VISITED

FAVOURITED

ROYAL ATTENDANT

THIS SAVVY QUEEN'S AIDE ALWAYS KNOWS HOW TO SAVE THE DAY

The faithful and trusty aide of Queen Teiyia, the Royal Attendant – known as Nimeway to her friends – is always on hand when the queen has an errand that needs running. But don't let her humble title fool you, she is more than just a glamorous personal assistant! On several occasions, she has saved Queen Teiyia from many a piratey predicament or ethereal mishap.

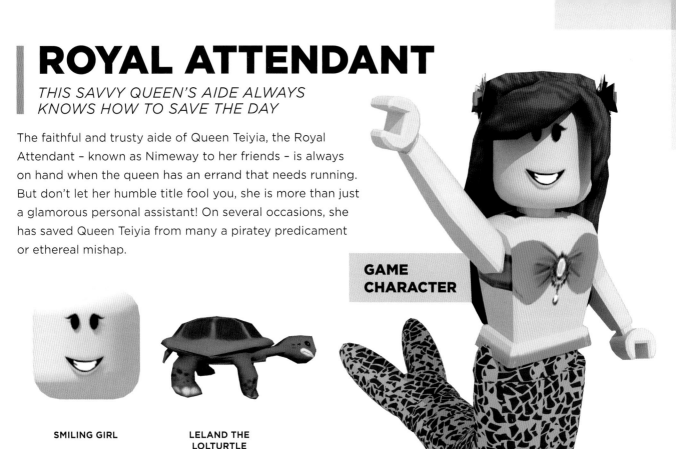

GAME CHARACTER

SMILING GIRL

LELAND THE LOLTURTLE

SERVING ROYALTY IN ... NEVERLAND LAGOON

GAME INFORMATION

Royal Attendant is based on Neverland Lagoon by developer SelDraken. It's an open-world experience where players can interact to create stories and adventures, featuring a huge map complete with a castle, pirate cove, native village and fairy pond. Players can customise their appearance with lots of clothes, accessories and morphs that transform their avatars into a range of mermaids, fairies or pirates.

DEVELOPER

SelDraken (p. 113) and Teiyia (p. 127)

VISITED

FAVOURITED

ROYSTANFORD

THERE'S ONLY ONE THING ON THIS ADVENTUROUS DEV'S MIND – SURVIVAL

An unparalleled survivalist with endurance and speed unlike any other Robloxian, RoyStanford has embraced the barbarous lifestyle by creating a series of games that truly test your mettle. Throughout his developing career, he has crafted games such as The Living Dead, Redwood Prison, Cops and Robbers, Zed Defense Tycoon and many, many more.

SHOULDER SLOTH   **SAFARI SLOUCH**

CREATOR

DEVELOPER TIMELINE

APRIL 2014
This proficient creator started work on his first foray into the criminal action genre Cops and Robbers, which has attracted over 3 million visits.

APRIL 2016
After a productive 2015, which saw the release of Patient Zero and The Living Dead, RoyStanford struck gold with his popular Redwood Prison.

AUGUST 2014
2014 proved to be a busy developmental year for RoyStanford, as he also started to craft the zombie-filled action game Zed Defense Tycoon.

JULY 2017
RoyStanford just kept creating and in the summer of 2017 he cooked up the addictive Bakers Valley, which has over 48 million visits to date.

SELDRAKEN

DASHING DEVELOPER OF MAGICAL ROBLOX ROLE-PLAY EXPERIENCES

This mysterious, horn-masked gamemaker is the developer behind the hugely popular role-play adventure game, Neverland Lagoon. Alongside fellow game creator Teiyia, SelDraken has delved deep into the fantastical depths of all things magical, from mermaids and fairies to lost treasures and swashbuckling pirates.

CREATOR

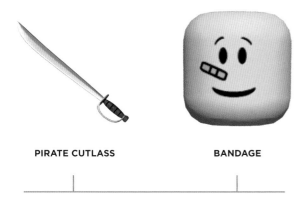

PIRATE CUTLASS   BANDAGE

DEVELOPER TIMELINE

JULY 2010
SelDraken had been a programmer for over a decade, but when he discovered Roblox, he started to explore the bold new bloxy frontier.

RBBLBX

JUL 2010

QUICK FACT
SelDraken is an avid outfit designer and has a whole range of clothes for sale in the Roblox Catalog.

MAY 2015
After five years of being entertained and inspired by the creative possibilities of Roblox, SelDraken started to create his open-world, role-play classic Neverland Lagoon.

QUICK FACT
SelDraken is the co-owner of the Mermaid and Pirate Neverland Lagoon fan group with fellow Robloxian Teiyia.

SERANOK

CONNOISSEUR OF COLLECTIBLES AND COLLECTIBLE-GAME CREATOR

Long-time Roblox superstar and brother of Merely, Seranok won the community's choice Player of the Year award in 2012, and is widely acclaimed for his work on the classic game Catalog Heaven. A lover of all things collectible, his much-lauded Golden Chalice of Fame allows him to exude pure illustriousness wherever he roams, while his Rocket Jumper propels him into the Robloxian stratosphere!

ROBLOX CLASSIC

STEAMPUNK SHADES

SERANOK GOLDEN CHALICE OF FAME

ONE OF HIS FAVOURITE GAMES IS ... CUBE EAT CUBE

After a hard day at Roblox HQ, this inventive programmer likes to unwind with even more blox-based fun in Stickmasterluke's classic Cube Eat Cube. This top-down battle game starts you and your opponents off as tiny cubes and tasks you with collecting and swallowing as many square-pellets as you can. Once you get big enough, the real fun begins as you gain the ability to swallow your smaller enemies. Yum!

GAME STATS

DEVELOPER
Stickmasterluke (p. 121)

This legendary game, which has garnered over 25 million plays, was created by Roblox staffer and dev extraordinaire Stickmasterluke, who is also responsible for The Underground War.

VISITED

FAVOURITED

SHADEOFBLUE

THE ULTIMATE FASHIONISTA, BUT CAN YOU GUESS HER SECRET IDENTITY?

This helpful attendant and confidante from Top Roblox Runway Model is more than an average NPC! Behind her fashion-conscious façade lies a backstory so dizzyingly glamorous and controversial that only her close-knit fashion friends know her secrets ... until now! She's always on hand to pass on style tips to contestants and turn them from fashion flops to catwalk royalty.

GAME CHARACTER

TEDDY BEAR HAT

KUDDLE E. KOALA

PUSHING PRODUCT IN ... RETAIL TYCOON

GAME INFORMATION

When ShadeOfBlue isn't handing out helpful fashion advice to avid stylistas in Top Roblox Runway Model, she is indulging in some retail therapy in Retail Tycoon. However, she's not content with just filling her bags, instead she runs her own empire of commerce, selling products ranging from crisps and fizzy drinks to collectible cars and unique jewellery. Customers flock in from all over Robloxia to visit her flagship store!

DEVELOPER
Haggie125 (p. 52)

VISITED

FAVOURITED

SHARKSIE

*HALF-MELON, HALF-SHARK
AND A WHOLE LOT OF FUN*

When this shark fanatic isn't out on the prowl for his next tasty treat, he's developing his own awesome games and experiences. Some of the greatest masterpieces Sharksie has sunk his developer teeth into include Tiny Tanks, Store Wars and Robloxian High School, which have a jaw-snapping total of more than 300 million plays!

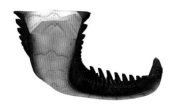

**WATERMELON
SHARK**

ALLIGATOR TAIL

CREATOR

DEVELOPER TIMELINE

JANUARY 2015
Sharksie started to work on the game that would eventually emerge as the frantic Tiny Tanks!, with a little help from supreme developer Gusmanak.

OCTOBER 2017
After forming the game development group Abstract Shark Games, Sharksie and the team released the stab-and-survive action game Knife Capsules.

JULY 2016
After a lesson or two in game creation, Sharksie cleared his timetable and started to get Robloxian High School ready for a new term of gamers.

QUICK FACT
Sharksie owns an Official Model Maker badge, meaning his creations are officially endorsed by Roblox!

RBXM

SHEDLETSKY

INTEGRAL COG IN THE ROBLOX MACHINE SINCE ITS INCEPTION

Shedletsky was one of the pioneering members of the Roblox team, and an early colleague of Builderman. He is known for being a formidable programmer and an expert jack-of-all-trades. One of the most useful strings to his bow are his impeccable rocket launcher skills, which are especially handy when trying to nuke a whale.

ROBLOX CLASSIC

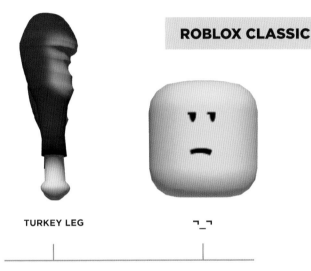

TURKEY LEG

¬_¬

ONE OF HIS FAVOURITE GAMES IS ... TINY TANKS!

This MVP of all things Roblox is more than just handy with a rocket launcher, he's pretty destructive with tiny things as well ... like toy tanks! Shedletsky likes to let off steam in Sharksie and Co.'s massively addictive combat game Tiny Tanks!. Players team up and guide their tanks through the variety of fun maps while looking to blow their foes to smithereens with some fancy trick shots and clever rebound blasts!

GAME STATS

DEVELOPER
Sharksie (p. 116)

Created by Robloxian regulars Sharksie, Gusmanak and NWSpacek, this fun team-battle game has notched up more than 19 million visits from tank fans aiming to dominate the minuscule maps.

VISITED

FAVOURITED

SHELLC

IMAGINATIVE GAMEMAKER AND INTEGRAL PART OF A 'TINY GAME STUDIO'

shellc is an innovative developer, known for original gameplay and clever game design. Teaming up with Numoji to bring gamers a unique experience, she released the multiplayer battle game Rollernauts. The game's inventiveness and striking art didn't go unnoticed, and they won a 2016 Bloxy Award for Best Mobile Design.

BUNNY SCARF

BEARY CHILLY BASEBALL CAP

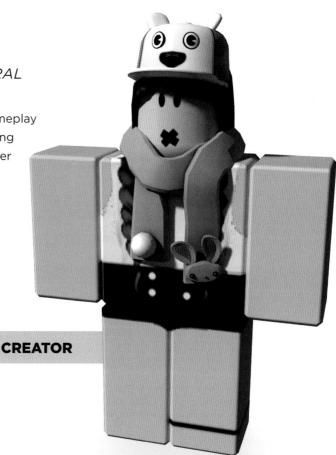

CREATOR

DEVELOPER TIMELINE

JANUARY 2016
This inventive developer finally found a home where she could come out of her shell and create awesome games. Where else but Roblox, of course.

ROBLOX

JAN 2016

FEBRUARY 2017
At the 4th annual Bloxy Awards, which recognised the best games of 2016, her collaboration with Numoji netted a Bloxy Award for Mobile Design.

JULY 2016
shellc joined forces with game studio Numoji to create the brilliant ball-battler Rollernauts, which has been enjoyed by over 7 million people so far.

QUICK FACT
shellc is known to help and support other game dev groups, such as Gusmanak's Dualpoint Interactive and Imaginaerum's Negative Games.

SKATERBOI

GNARLY DUDE MORE COMFORTABLE ON FOUR WHEELS THAN TWO LEGS

Skaterboi knows all the tricks in the manual and then some! He can pull off a gnarly 720 flip into a rail grind without breaking a sweat, and more importantly, he does it with a grungy air of effortless cool. Wherever Skaterboi goes, so does his board, mainly to the skate park where he hangs out, practises tricks and impresses his fellow skaters!

ROBLOX FAMILY CHARACTER

): RED GRIND

RED GRIND SKATEBOARD

CAUSING A RUCKUS IN ... CAR CRUSHERS

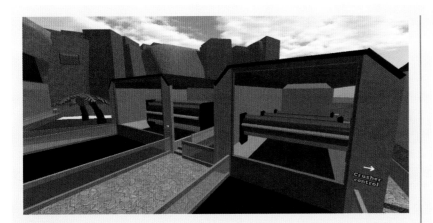

Skaterboi has a need for speed and is full to the brim with teenage angst, so he likes to deal with both urges at once in his all-time favourite Roblox game Car Crushers. Skaterboi finds it relaxing to drive around at top speed, before zooming off to his favourite crushing machine and watching the car get decimated! The more expensive the car is, the better.

GAME STATS

DEVELOPER
Panwellz

Developer Panwellz is the driving force behind Car Crushers, and his game of destruction has gained over 335,000 favourites from auto demolition fans! He also released a sequel in early 2017.

VISITED

FAVOURITED

SKYBOUND ADMIRAL

SEASONED VETERAN OF THE SKYWAYS, PROLIFIC IN AERIAL COMBAT

This intrepid explorer rose to the rank of Admiral after decades of adventure in Imaginaerum's Skybound 2. His epic escapades have led him and his crew on a never-ending quest for treasure in the sky, where he has got into a few sticky situations. However, the Skybound Admiral's cunning tends to help him find his way out of trouble ... one way or another.

GAME CHARACTER

STEAMPUNK WINGS OF MECHANICAL DESTINY

ADMIRAL OF THE ROYAL SKYFLEET

COMMANDING THE FLEET IN ... SKYBOUND 2

GAME INFORMATION

This sky-high commander originates from adventure epic Skybound 2. Set among a realm of floating islands, players captain their own flying ship and roam the skies looking for skirmishes. Islands can be conquered, treasures discovered and alliances forged, giving players resources to buy better ships and weapons. The game is open-ended and perfect for epic battles, which is why it has attracted over 20 million visits.

DEVELOPER
Imaginaerum

VISITED

FAVOURITED

STICKMASTERLUKE

*PROLIFIC DEVELOPER OF MULTIPLE
ROBLOX MASTERPIECES*

He's the master of disaster and a
born survivor with a penchant for
medieval headwear. Antlers have
never gone out of fashion, right?
Just ask Rudolph! Stickmasterluke
has forged some of the most popular
games on Roblox, including the
thunderous Natural Disaster Survival, the
subterranean The Underground War and the
tasty Cube Eat Cube.

ROBLOX CLASSIC

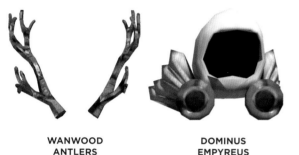

**WANWOOD
ANTLERS**

**DOMINUS
EMPYREUS**

ONE OF HIS FAVOURITE GAMES IS ... WELCOME TO BLOXBURG

As a longstanding member of the Roblox community, Stickmasterluke
loves nothing more than making new friends, and he's found the perfect
game to take his social life to a new level: Welcome to Bloxburg. Citizens of
Bloxburg can claim their own home, decorate and stock it exactly to their
liking, and invite the rest of the neighbourhood over for a party! He's been
welcoming friends to his pad ever since the game was released in 2014.

GAME STATS

DEVELOPER
Coeptus

Coeptus has worked on Welcome to
Bloxburg for over four years, adding
features for over 170 million citizens
ever since its release. It has received
many Bloxys, including one for
Favourite Updated Game.

VISITED

FAVOURITED

SUPER BOMB SURVIVAL SHOPGIRL

WHAT SHE DOESN'T STOCK ISN'T WORTH TAKING INTO THE ARENA

If you ever find yourself under a barrage of bombs falling from the sky, don't panic! Super Bomb Survival Shopgirl has got just the thing to make your life a megaton easier ... as long as you have the credits. She's quite the entrepreneurial dynamo and has served over 59 million customers and counting!

GAME CHARACTER

MAKE IT RAIN

RED CURLY PIGTAILS

A BILLION SERVED IN ... SUPER BOMB SURVIVAL

GAME INFORMATION

This savvy Shopgirl is always willing to do business in Polyhex's explosive hit Super Bomb Survival, which has been favourited over half a million times. Players must strive to survive two and a half minutes in the arena, as destruction rains down from above. There are lots of maps and a wealth of bombs with different characteristics. Between rounds players can buy special skills and perks to help them survive.

DEVELOPER
Polyhex

VISITED

FAVOURITED

SUPER HERO LIFE: STARLASS

STAR-POWERED SCOURGE OF SUPERVILLAINS EVERYWHERE

After encountering radioactive material emanating from a mysterious comet, Starlass gained incredible super powers that gave her enhanced strength, healing and the ability to fly at the speed of light. Together with her adorably feisty feline sidekick, she uses her exceptional fighting skills to bring justice and peace to the world in Super Hero Life!

GAME CHARACTER

ASTRAL ISLES WARRIOR HAIR

SHOULDER SHARK CAT

SAVING THE DAY IN ... SUPER HERO LIFE

GAME INFORMATION

Starlass is based on the all-action RPG Super Hero Life, which has had more than 27 million visits. Gamers get to play as a hero of their own making, design their very own super-suit and choose their weapons and powers. They can even customise their character with a civilian alter ego! Once the origin story is complete, players must decide whether to follow a path of righteousness and justice, or pursue a life of crime and villainy.

DEVELOPER
CJ_Oyer

VISITED

FAVOURITED

SWAT UNIT

ELITE PURSUER OF JUSTICE THAT DOESN'T NEED A PLAN B

When chaos erupts in the prison, and the inmates are breaking loose, there's only one man who can handle the job ... SWAT Unit. Trained in the art of riot control, this agent is the master of crisis management and will make sure the bad guys are back behind bars before lights-out.

RIOT SHIELD AND BILLY CLUB SET

AWKWARD EYEROLL

KEEPING IT LOCKED DOWN IN ... PRISON LIFE

GAME INFORMATION

The SWAT Unit is one of several wielders of justice inspired by Prison Life, created by award-winning developer Aesthetical. As elite prison guards in the game, players must stop inmates escaping from jail, with a surveillance room and armoury to help them keep control. Guards can upgrade to riot gear with the correct game passes, and there's a range of guns and tools. But beware: everything a guard has, the inmates want!

DEVELOPER
Aesthetical (p. 7)

VISITED

FAVOURITED

TEAISM

*HE MAY BE BLUE, BUT THERE'S
NOBODY MORE CHILLED OUT*

This cooler-than-cool, icier-than-iced-tea developer is a
long-time Roblox veteran and is known for directing the
classic Roblox strategy card game, BLOX Cards. When
Teaism isn't chilling out and quenching his thirst with iced
tea in his Icy Café, then you'll probably find him playing it
cool and levelling-up his supreme card-battling skills.

CREATOR

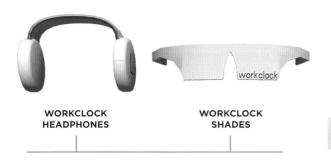

**WORKCLOCK
HEADPHONES**

**WORKCLOCK
SHADES**

DEVELOPER TIMELINE

JULY 2010
A month after joining
Roblox, this cool customer
opened the doors to his own
place, The IcyCafe, where
Robloxians could flock to
chill out.

JUNE 2016
In collaboration with
ByDefault, Teaism's I-C-T
Studios created the absurdly
extraordinary building game,
Obstacle Paradise, which has
since garnered 4 million visits.

JULY 2015
After five years on Roblox,
Teaism revealed the next
entry in his development
arsenal, the awesome and
addictive card-strategy
game BLOX Cards.

JULY 2017
Diving into a world of chance
and randomness, Teaism
began working on The Case
Game with the fellow devs of
Cornea Games, which opened
its doors in Summer 2017.

TEE VEES PIZZA LOVER

CHAMPION OF THE ARCADE AND PILLAR OF THE PIZZA PARLOUR

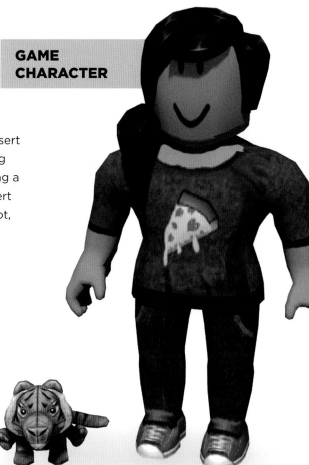

This girl loves one thing: pizza. If she were stranded on a desert island and she could only bring three things, she would bring pizza, pizza, and her little tiger friend, who also loves mauling a slice of pepperoni! But would she ever find herself on a desert island? No way, she's always hanging at her number-one spot, Tee & Vee's Pizza and Arcade!

BLACK PONYTAIL

TIGER FRIEND

QUEUING UP FOR A SLICE IN ... TEE & VEE'S PIZZA AND ARCADE

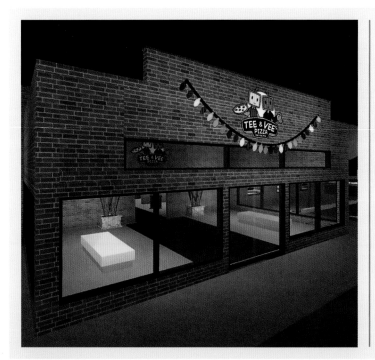

GAME INFORMATION

This food-fanatic calls Tee & Vee's Pizza and Arcade home. It's one of the longest-running role-play experiences on Roblox, in which you can visit a pizza parlour, check the menu and order your favourite pizza. There's also a cool arcade with a dance floor and fun games to play, with lots of prizes to be claimed. Originally created in 2008 by developer KxraDraws, the game was relaunched in 2015 to a new generation of fans.

DEVELOPER
KxraDraws

VISITED

FAVOURITED

TEIYIA

CHARISMATIC CREATOR AND ENTHUSIAST OF ALL THINGS GAMING

This ethereal developer is best known for creating the ever-popular role-playing game Neverland Lagoon. She is the authority on all things mythical and magical, and she sprinkles her fairy dust on all her creations. Teiyia is also an avid gamer and loves to flutter between her most-loved Roblox games.

CREATOR

NEON PARTY CROWN

INTERSTELLAR WINGS

DEVELOPER TIMELINE

MID 2010
Teiyia joined Roblox and started playing games with her kids and husband. Together they've enjoyed many hours of family gaming fun!

LATE 2017
She worked on the latest revamp for Neverland Lagoon, with a view of releasing a reboot with new maps, characters, GUI and role-play features!

EARLY 2015
Teiyia opened the Roblox Studio for the first time and began playing around with the myriad tools. She ended up with a magical world ... the rest is Neverland history!

EARLY 2018
Not content with just building fantastical terrains, Teiyia started to widen her programming knowledge and added to her already superb sculpting skills.

THEGAMER101

ACCUMULATOR OF ROBLOXIAN ANTIQUITIES AND RARITIES

After spending years honing his sword-fighting skills, TheGamer101 fears no sabre-bearing warrior! It's not in this Roblox staffer's personality to shy away from an epic battle, so he continues to train by battling stronger and more fearsome foes. TheGamer101 also loves to trade Robloxian wares and is always on the lookout for rare and limited-edition treasures.

ROBLOX CLASSIC

BLACK IRON DOMINO CROWN OF INTERNS

GOLD FLASH SHADES

ONE OF HIS FAVOURITE GAMES IS ... KNIFE CAPSULES

TheGamer101 likes to put his knife-mastery skills to the test in the free-for-all combat game Knife Capsules. Players must hunt down their target across a number of awesome maps, and try to be the last player standing. The rounds are frantic, and often dominated by those who can find the best hiding places to launch their knives in secret. Winners receive gold, which can be used to buy capsules, which in turn can be redeemed in the lobby for a brand new deadly weapon.

GAME STATS

DEVELOPER

Abstract Shark Games

This dev group is full of superstar creators, including Sharksie, AbstractAlex, RedMantaStudios, and TheStoreOpens. Knife Capsules was their first release in early 2017, and has been visited 10 million times.

VISITED

FAVOURITED

TIM7775, REDGUARD

LEGENDARILY ELUSIVE CREATOR; YOU'LL ONLY SEE HIM IF HE WANTS YOU TO

All hail the enchanted Knight of Redcliff! This developer bears the wings of an angel and the mind of a master programmer, and he is ready to descend from the sky to save Robloxia from the great Korblox army. When he's not combatting evil, Tim7775 is usually working on one of the most popular Roblox games, Hide and Seek Extreme.

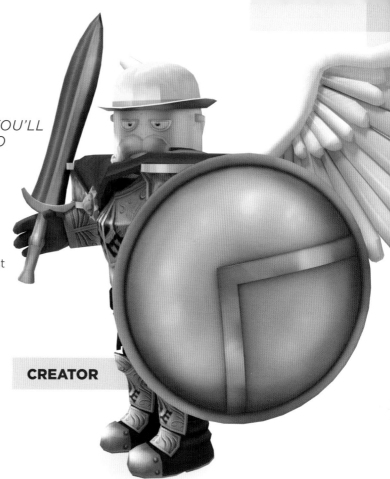

CREATOR

SPARTAN SWORD AND SHIELD

DONALD P. SULLIVAN – GOLD EDITION

DEVELOPER TIMELINE

OCTOBER 2011
After a couple of years refining his talents for all things Roblox, Tim7775 celebrated success in the 2009 and 2011 Halloween Paintball events, claiming two trophies.

JUNE 2015
Taking a break from fighting the evil Korblox empire, Tim7775 crafted the epic building game Building Frenzy, which has recently been remastered.

JANUARY 2015
Tim7775's awesome game creation skills came out of hiding and he showed the Roblox world what he could do with his hit game Hide and Seek Extreme.

QUICK FACT
Hide and Seek Extreme has amassed a huge following and has been visited more than 200 million times!

UNCLE SAM'S UNCLE

RED, WHITE AND BLUE, HIS COLOURS RUN THROUGH

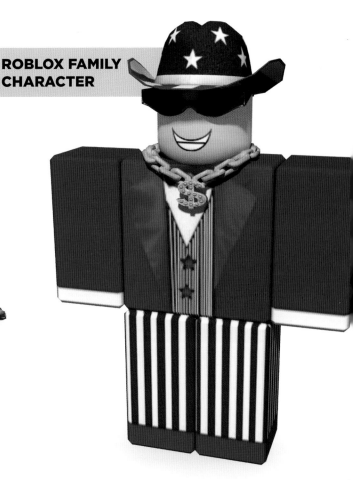

Red-blooded, with a cool-blue sensibility and white-hot passion for patriotism ... it's Uncle Sam's Uncle. He's got a lot of respect for his nephew, but let's face it, he's the real American hero. Soaring high over the frontier plains on a bald eagle, Uncle Sam's Uncle allows liberty to ring across a nation as they dream the American Dream.

AMERICAN COWBOY

BLING $$ NECKLACE

ELIMINATING PLAYERS WITH PATRIOTIC PRECISION IN ... DODGEBALL!

This star-spangled relative is a big fan of the American classic DODGEBALL! by talented developer Alexnewtron. It's a fast-paced elimination game full of dodging, ducking, dipping and diving. When the balls start flying, you better hope that he's on your team, because he will give his all for his team and his country. U-S-A! U-S-A!

GAME STATS

DEVELOPER
Alexnewtron (p. 9)

DODGEBALL! was one of the first games that Alexnewtron released on Roblox, and it's been visited by over 40 million sports fans. His other games include MeepCity, the first game to reach a billion visits!

VISITED

FAVOURITED

V_YRISS

CATACLYSMS, CATASTROPHES AND CALAMITIES ARE HER BREAD AND BUTTER

A natural-born artist and developer, V_yriss made her claim to fame on Roblox by creating the mega-popular Survive the Disasters series! She's reigned supreme as the queen of catastrophe since joining Roblox in 2009, and her creations have been visited more than 150 million times since then!

CREATOR

PIRATE CAPTAIN'S HAT

POLAR BEAR SHOULDER FRIEND

DEVELOPER FACTS

QUICK FACT

V_yriss joined the world of Robloxia in January 2009, and set about unleashing her cataclysmic trilogy of Survive the Disasters adventure games on the community.

JAN 2009

QUICK FACT

V_yriss is the proud owner of the Bloxxer Badge, awarded to players with over 250 victories in a classic Roblox game. It's now unattainable on Roblox!

250

QUICK FACT

V_yriss is a connoisseur of collectible items, and has dozens of them in her collection, including the legendary headpiece, Dominus Messor.

QUICK FACT

V_yriss is sometimes known as TheFurryFox and is the owner of the popular community fan group TheFurryFox Fans, which has 5,000 members.

VORLIAS

DEVELOPER FROM DOWN UNDER AT THE TOP OF HIS GAME

A legendary hero from New Sealaan, Vorlias's almighty programming power has led to the creation of an entire world known as Zenerith. As the lead developer on Heroes' Legacy, this epic developer and his heroic team at Aurora Australis are steadily building a sprawling role-playing game filled with larger-than-life battles and perilous quests.

WALRUS

CONDUCTOR'S GOLD
POCKET WATCH

CREATOR

DEVELOPER TIMELINE

AUGUST 2009
Lost for things to do in New Zealand, Vorlias decided it was the right time to harness his gaming skills and unleash his programming prowess on the Roblox platform.

ROBLOX
AUG 2009

SEPTEMBER 2015
With the world of Zenerith planned in immaculate detail in his head, Vorlias started to make it a gaming reality as he built his new game, Heroes' Legacy.

JANUARY 2010
Vorlias began to forge his epic legacy saga and created the first entry in the series, known simply as Legacy, which was updated as recently as 2017.

QUICK FACT
The Heroes' Legacy fan group has a heroic membership of over 1,400 Robloxians.

VURSE

RENOWNED CREATOR WITH A PRODIGIOUS PASSION FOR PACE

The high-flying and much-celebrated Vurse is a legendary developer whose awesome scripting mastery has earned him multiple Bloxy Awards for his flagship Roblox game, Speed Run 4. Not only did he capture the community's choice award for the hardest Roblox level, but he also won the much-coveted accolade for best single-player game!

CREATOR

DOMINUS FRIGIDUS

MAJESTIC ICE WING

DEVELOPER TIMELINE

OCTOBER 2014
Just eighteen months after joining Roblox, Vurse began to pick up the pace and released Speed Run 4, the confusingly numbered first entry in his popular series.

MAY 2015
Vurse released Speed Run Reloaded, which took the same insanely hard obby formula and put it in a variety of brand new and exciting settings.

MAY 2015
Vurse enhanced the Speed Run 4 experience by crafting the topsy-turvy 'impossible' version of the game. He even encouraged angry comments about the game's difficulty!

QUICK FACT
Vurse is known in the game developer community for his support of other developers' games and has been a tester on many classic Roblox hits.

ZKEVIN

ECCENTRIC CLEANING ENTHUSIAST AND MULTI-SKILLED GAME AUTEUR

If you step into the world of zKevin's wild and wicked imagination, you'll be in for the ride of your life! This awesome Roblox developer is renowned across the Roblox community for his quirky, inventive creations and is the man behind the zany and madcap adventures in classic Roblox games such as Purple Skittles, Cube Cavern, Cleaning Simulator and Blamo.

CREATOR

PLUNGER SWORDPACK

PASTEL RAINBOW SHAGGY

DEVELOPER TIMELINE

JULY 2011
zKevin stepped forth from his own wacky world and into the wild land of Roblox game development with Burger Aboard!, a burger sim with added physics!

SEPTEMBER 2016
Moving on from Purple Skittles, this imaginative developer created the 3D adventure game, Blamo, which pushed game design to a strange new place.

FEBRUARY 2016
With so many quirky ideas to make a reality, zKevin added to his peculiar portfolio with the fun adventure-puzzle game Purple Skittles.

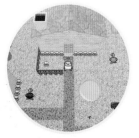

MAY 2017
After giving his mind a spring cleaning, zKevin had a brain-tsunami and created the hugely popular Cleaning Simulator, which is hiding more than a few secrets.

ZOMBIE RUSHER

ON A FIENDISH HUNT, HE'S COMING TO GET YOU ... JUST QUITE SLOWLY

The easiest and quickest way to kill a zombie is an accurate headshot to the ... head. But not against this Zombie Rusher! He's one stumbling step ahead of the game. His helmet protects him from sharpshooting snipers, lucky gunslingers and close-range spanner swipes. Unfortunately for this zombie, his hard-hat of protection is quite heavy and makes him more cumbersome than normal, which for a zombie means he's really, really, really, really slow.

GAME CHARACTER

SAD ZOMBIE

OPERATION DESERT CYCLONE

RUSHING SURVIVORS IN ... APOCALYPSE RISING 2

GAME INFORMATION

In his leisure time, this Zombie Rusher likes to spawn into Apocalypse Rising 2, a super-sequel created by Dualpoint Interactive. It's a dangerous place for a zombie to exist, as players hunt and scavenge to survive, sometimes at the expense of other players or the poor, hungry zombies. But that doesn't stop Zombie Rusher – he loves to amble through the wide world, and there are plenty of places to hide if he gets in danger.

DEVELOPER
Dualpoint Interactive

VISITED

FAVOURITED

ZOMBIE RUSHER

'HANGRY' FOR BRAINS, ALL THIS ZOMBIE RUSHER WANTS IS HIS NEXT SNACK

GRRRRR! This undead fiend is just ... misunderstood. He's not angry, he's just hungry! The trouble is his insatiable appetite for Robloxian brains, flesh and bones means he is always 'hangry'. And an end-of-the-world apocalypse doesn't help matters. Now his favourite snacks are rushing around with knives, guns, and makeshift weapons, not to mention hiding in hard-to-reach places.

GAME CHARACTER

FRYING PAN

BEAUTIFUL BROWN HAIR FOR BEAUTIFUL PEOPLE

EATS BRAINS EVERY DAY IN ... ZOMBIE RUSH

GAME INFORMATION

This undead fellow is one of many hungry fiends from the popular horror combat game Zombie Rush, created by HomingBeacon and his fellow devs at Beacon Studio. Players choose an eerie map to survive in, and are armed with a gun, a melee weapon and their survival wits. Players must kill as many zombies as they can before the horde overwhelms their defences, and Zombie Rusher and his pals get to have a Robloxian feast!

DEVELOPER
Beacon Studio

VISITED

FAVOURITED

COLLECTOR'S GUIDE

So you're acquainted with characters native to every corner of Robloxia, from the YouTube sensations and industrious staffers, to exciting game characters and exceptionally talented devs. But did you know that you can own every character featured in this book?

Roblox has partnered with toy company Jazwares, and the pair have created a collection of official figures encompassing the most exciting characters on the platform. There are mystery figures, playsets based on the most popular games, mix & match sets that allow you to create your own characters and much more. You even get an exclusive virtual item with every toy you purchase!

This Collector's Guide lists every single toy that's been released in the first three waves, so you can see how complete your collection is and which figures you need to hunt down next!

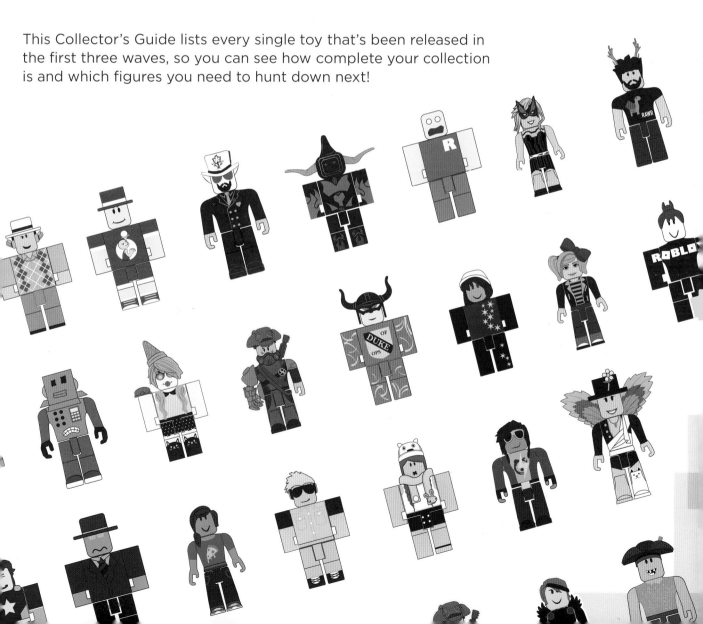

MYSTERY FIGURES

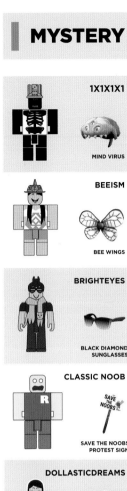 **1X1X1X1**

MIND VIRUS

 AESTHETICAL

SILVER BOW TIE

 ALEXNEWTRON

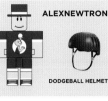

DODGEBALL HELMET

ASIMO3089

WHITE SWORD CANE

AZUREWRATH, LORD OF THE VOID

AZUREWRATH'S ADDITIONAL HEAD HORNS

BEEISM

BEE WINGS

BEREZAA

AZURE MINES PICKAXE

BLOGGIN ALL CATS

STITCHFRIENDS: CUTE CAT

BLUESTEEL WARRIOR

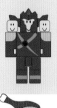

BLUESTEEL WARRIOR'S HEADBAND

BOY GUEST

ROBLOX VISOR #2

BRIGHTEYES

BLACK DIAMOND SUNGLASSES

BUILDERMAN

CEO WRENCHPACK

BUSINESS CAT

BUSINESS CAT'S BUSINESS BRIEFCASE

CHICKEN MAN

COTM: OCTEMBER ENCORE

CINDERING

SHOULDER DEV: CINDERING

CLASSIC NOOB

SAVE THE NOOBS PROTEST SIGN

CLUB NYONIC: SINGER

GOLD MICROPHONE

DEFAULTIO

GLAMOROUS ROCKSTAR HAIR

DIGGIN ALL DOGS

STITCHFRIENDS: DIGNIFIED DOG

DIZZYPURPLE

PURPLE TRAFFIC CONE

DOLLASTICDREAMS

THE RIGHT TO REMAIN FABULOUS

DORM LIFE: PEER COUNSELOR

ROBLOX U BASEBALL CAP

DUED1

SHOULDER DEV: DUED1

EPIC MINER

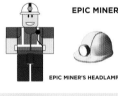

EPIC MINER'S HEADLAMP

ERIK.CASSEL

ERIK'S CODE REVIEW SPECS

EVILARTIST

INTERSTELLAR RABBIT EARS

EZEBEL: THE PIRATE QUEEN

EZEBEL'S JEWELED EYEPATCH

FIREBRAND1

PURPLE SPECTOLOUPES

FRAMED: SPY

TOTALLY NOT A SPY

FUZZYWOOO

NOOB ATTACK: SHARK SITUATION

GALAXY GIRL

NAVY QUEEN OF THE NIGHT

GEEGEE92

EMERALD ANIMAZING HAIR

GIRL GUEST

ROBLOX VISOR #1

HAGGIE125

COPPER BOTTOM POT

INITIATE OF GLORIOUS FLIGHT

SHOULDER OWL

KEITH

EXECUTIVE BLACK IRON TENTACLES

LANDO64000

SCARLET LAPEL FLOWER

LET'S MAKE A DEAL

SHARK FIN

LILLY_S

LADY OF THE FEDERATION NECKLACE

MAELSTRONOMER

RED HEADSTACK

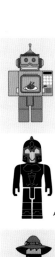

MICROWAVE SPYBOT

MICROWAVE SPY EYE

MR. ROBOT

BACKUP MR. ROBOT

MYZTA

BLAZING MIDNIGHT SHADES

NEXX

NEXX LEVEL GUITAR

NOOB007

MANTLE OF THE DARK LORD OF SQL

NOOBERTUBER

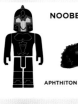

APHTHITON PAULDRONS

OFFICER ZOMBIE

ZOMBIE FIREMAN

PIXELATEDCANDY

HOT PINK 8BIT HEADPHONES

PLAYROBOT

JADE ROBOT CHARM NECKLACE

PYROLYSIS

FIRE TIE

QUENTY

8 BIT BANDANA

REESEMCBLOX

RAINBOW UNICORN BEANIE

RIPULL

EMERALD NOOBFINDERS

ROBLOX STAFF

8 BIT CONSTRUCTION HELMET

ROBLOX SUPER FAN

ROBLOX "R" SUNGLASSES

ROBLOX UNIVERSITY PROFESSOR

SUPER SPEEDY PINK POTION

ROBLOX UNIVERSITY STUDENT

RU COURSE CATALOG

ROCKSTAR

CLASSIC ROCKSTAR LOOK

ROYSTANFORD

SHOULDER RACCOON

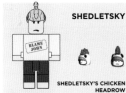

SHARKSIE

WATERMELON SHARK FIN

SHEDLETSKY

SHEDLETSKY'S CHICKEN HEADROW

SHELLC

BLACK HAIR WITH TEAL BOWS

SKATERBOI

): RED GRIND ORIGINAL FLYER SKATEBOARD

STICKMASTERLUKE

STICKPACK

SUPER BOMB SURVIVAL SHOPGIRL

JUST A BOMB GIRL

SUPER HERO LIFE: STARLASS

STARLASS SUPERHERO CAPE

TEAISM

ICY TEA TIE

TEE VEES PIZZA LOVER

PIZZA INFINITY SCARF

UNCLE SAM'S UNCLE

AMERICAN BASEBALL CAP

V_YRISS

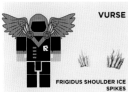

DISASTER SURVIVAL HELMET

VURSE

FRIGIDUS SHOULDER ICE SPIKES

ZKEVIN

PUKA SHELL NECKLACE

CORE FIGURES

BLUE LAZER PARKOUR RUNNER

BLUE LAZER SWORD

BRIDE

BLUE DIAMOND TIARA

CAPTAIN RAMPAGE

SHOULDER MONKEY

CIRCUIT BREAKER

EVIL ROBOT HEAD

HANG GLIDER

BUBBLEGUM BOMBER

HUNTED VAMPIRE

BITEYMCFACE

LORD UMBERHALLOW

UMBERHORNS

MATT DUSEK

BLADE OF THE DUSEKKAR

MEEPCITY FISHERMAN

MEEP HAT

MR. BLING BLING

GREEN ROBUX TOP HAT

PHANTOM FORCES: GHOST

BLUE GHOST BERET

PIXEL ARTIST

ALOOF ARTIST BERET

QUEEN OF THE TREELANDS

AUTUMN CLOAK OF ALL THINGS ENDING

ROBLOX SKATING RINK

ALUMINIUM SELFIE STICK

SKYBOUND ADMIRAL

SKYBOUND GUNBLADE

TEIYIA

DREAMER CAP

TIM7775, REDGUARD

REDCLIFF HERO CAPE

VORLIAS

SIGNED, SEALED, DELIVERED

6-PACK ASSORTMENT

GUSMANAK

LITOZINNAMON

LOLERIS

MERELY

SERANOK

THEGAMER101

KORBLOX DEATHSPEAKER

KORBLOX MAGE

KORBLOX GENERAL

THE OVERSEER

REDCLIFF ELITE COMMANDER

ALAR, KNIGHT OF THE SPLINTERED SKIES

ITEMS

LEGENDS OF ROBLOX

THE GOLDEN ROBLOXIAN

CHAMPIONS OF ROBLOX

RICHARD, REDCLIFF KING

CHASERS

ADURITE SWORDPACK

BLACK CRYSTAL CIRCLET

GNARWHAL

THE WINGS OF IMAGINATION

JADE KATANA SWORDPACK

**KERNEL PANIC KATANA
(1X1X1X1'S)**

GOLDLIKA: ROBLOX

SHOULDER TIGER

**CLOAK OF DREAMS
UNBOUND**

**CLOCKWORK'S
GODDESS GAZERS**

WANWOOD SWORD CANE

GOLD BEE WINGS

**GOLD PLATED
SELFIE STICK**

**INEFFECTIVE ROCKSTAR
DISGUISE**

**SAPPHIRE
GLITZ HAIR**

FAMOUS AT 18

**WINGS OF DREAMS
UNBOUND**

GOLD DUST WINGS

**STITCHFRIENDS:
HAPPY HIPPO**

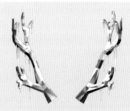

**FROZEN ANTLERS
OF EVERFROST**

MIX & MATCH

PUNK ROCKERS

FASHION ICONS

GAME PACKS

WORK AT A PIZZA PLACE

ROBLOX HIGH SCHOOL

MAD STUDIO MAD PACK

PRISON LIFE

TOP ROBLOX RUNWAY MODEL

VEHICLES

**NEIGHBORHOOD OF
ROBLOXIA PATROL CAR**

APOCALYPSE RISING 4X4

COLLECTOR'S TOOL BOX

COLLECTOR'S TOOL BOX

PLAYSETS

ZOMBIE ATTACK!

CONTAINS:

- ZOMBIE RUSHERS X2
- APOCALYPSE RISING: SURVIVOR
- NEIGHBORHOOD OF ROBLOXIA: MAYOR

NEVERLAND LAGOON

CONTAINS:

- NEVERLAND LAGOON: TEIYIA
- SELDRAKEN
- ROYAL ATTENDANT
- BUCK-EYE THE PIRATE

A GUIDE TO SOCIALISING ONLINE WITH ROBLOX

YOUNGER FANS' GUIDE TO ROBLOX

Spending time online is great fun! Roblox might be your first experience of digital socialising, so here are a few simple rules to help you stay safe and keep the internet a great place to spend time.

- Never give out your real name. Don't use your real name as your username.

- Never give out any of your personal details.
- Never tell anybody which school you go to or how old you are.
- Never tell anybody your password except a parent or guardian.
- Always tell a parent or guardian if something is worrying you.

PARENTS' GUIDE TO ROBLOX

Roblox has security and privacy settings that enable you to monitor and limit your child's access to the social features on Roblox, or turn them off completely. You can also limit the range of games your child can access, view their activity histories and report inappropriate activity on the site. Instructions for how to use these safety features are listed below.

NAVIGATING ROBLOX'S SAFETY FEATURES

To restrict your child from playing, chatting and messaging with others on Roblox, log in to your child's account and click on the **gear icon** in the upper right-hand corner of the site and select **Settings**. From here you can access the **Security** and **Privacy** menus:

- Users register for Roblox with their date of birth. It's important for children to enter the correct date because Roblox has default security and privacy settings that vary based on a player's age. This can be checked and changed in **Settings**.

- To review and restrict your child's social settings, go to **Settings** and select **Privacy**. Review the options under **Contact Settings** and **Other Settings**. Select **No one** or **Everyone**. Note: players age 13 and older have additional options.

- To control the safety features that are implemented on your child's account, you'll need to set up a 4-digit PIN. This will lock all of the settings, only enabling changes once the PIN is entered. To enable an Account PIN, go to the **Settings** page, select **Security**, and turn **Account PIN** to **ON**.

To help monitor your child's account, you can view the history for certain activities:

- To view your child's private message history, choose **Messages** from the menu bar down the left-hand side of the main screen. If the menu bar isn't visible, click on the list icon in the left-hand corner.

- To view your child's chat history with other players, open the **Chat & Party** window, located in the bottom-right of the page. Once this window is opened, you can click on any of the listed users to open a window with the chat history of that particular account.

- To view your child's online friends and followers, choose **Friends** from the menu bar down the left-hand side of the main screen.

- To view your child's creations, such as games, items, trades and sounds, choose **Develop** from the tabs running along the top of the main screen.

- To view any virtual items purchased and any trade history, choose **Trade** from the menu bar down the left-hand side of the main screen, then go to **My Transactions.**

While the imagery on Roblox has a largely blocky, digitised look, parents should be aware that some of the user-generated games may include themes or imagery that may be too intense for young or sensitive players:

- You can limit your child's account to display only a restricted list of available games to play. Go to **Settings**, select **Security**, and turn on **Account Restrictions.**

Roblox players of all ages have their posts and chats filtered to prevent personal information being shared, but no filter is foolproof. Roblox asks users and parents to report any inappropriate activity. Check your child's account and look to see if they have friends they do not know, and talk to your child about what to report (including bullying, inappropriate behaviour or messages, scams and other game violations):

- To report concerning behaviour on Roblox, players and parents can use the **Report Abuse** links located on game, group and user pages and in the **Report** tab of every game menu.

- To block another player during a game session: find the user on the leaderboard/player list at the upper-right of the game screen. (If the leaderboard/player list isn't there, open it by clicking on your username in the upper-right corner.) From here, click on the player you wish to block and select **Block User.**

For further information and help, Roblox has created a parents' guide to the website which can be accessed at https://corp.roblox.com/parents